When It All
Falls Down

When It All Falls Down

Dijorn Moss

www.urbanchristianonline.com

Urban Books, LLC
97 N18th Street
Wyandanch, NY 11798

When It All Falls Down Copyright © 2013 Dijorn Moss

ISBN 13: 978-1-60162-767-4
ISBN 10: 1-60162-767-X

First Printing September 2013
Printed in the United States of America

10 9 8 7 6 5 4 3 2 1

*This is a work of fiction. Any references or similarities
to actual events, real people, living or dead, or to real
locales are intended to give the novel a sense of reality.
Any similarity in other names, characters, places, and
incidents is entirely coincidental.*

Distributed by Kensington Corp.
Submit Wholesale Orders to:
Kensington Publishing Corp.
C/O Penguin Group (USA) Inc.
Attention: Order Processing
405 Murray Hill Parkway
East Rutherford, NJ 07073-2316
Phone: 1-800-526-0275
Fax: 1-800-227-9604

When It All
Falls Down

by

Dijorn Moss

To Trinea,

the woman who inspires me
to go to the next level.

To Caleb,

every day with you is a gift.

Acknowledgments

I first and foremost acknowledge my Lord and Savior Jesus Christ. Over the past few years you have led me through a fiery trail, but I have learned not to mourn over the things that was consumed by the fire, instead I celebrate what survived. I am a better man as a result. I also want to take the time to acknowledge the saints who God called home. To my grandmother, Doreatha Moss, who brought excellence to every endeavor and I miss our conversations. To Trina Kizzie, you are a strong woman who raised my wife to be a strong woman as well. I am forever grateful for your life and legacy.

To my parents: Mom, Dad, Elainna, and David, I love you all dearly and I now have a better understanding of the sacrifices you have made as parents. To my heroes Aunt Mary and Jovan Johnson, you inspire me to keep pushing even when it seems hopeless. To my brothers and sisters, Mike Boykins, Jaton Gunter, Mike Jacques, Sean Fritz, Alisha Carmen, and Dominique Williams, my life has been enriched as a result of knowing you.

To my spiritual homes: City of Refuge, Bible Way Christian Center, and Alondra Church of Christ, my walk with the Lord would not be as strong if it were not for you. To my editor Joy, we really partnered with the Holy Spirit and produced a great story. I am thankful for you always pushing me to be a better writer.

Acknowledgments

Finally, to you the reader. Thank you for purchasing this book and taking this journey with me. I hope that you will find this book thought-provoking, entertaining, and spiritually uplifting. Enjoy!

Chapter One

"Where is he now?" God asked Adam a similar question. While God's question dealt with the spiritual proximity of His and Adam's relationship, I literally want to know where is Charles Lewis, the senior pastor of True Vine Baptist Church, at 11:36 P.M. on a Friday night? We search every square inch of this 2,000-square-foot luxury hotel room and the only thing I can find is a broken condom wrapper, a bottle of Cristal that is starting to sweat, and a smell of unabashed sex that reaches up to the top of the Baltic ceiling and spreads from one end of the room to the next.

At the edge of the bed, a young girl in an overpriced scarlet corset sits with her face in her hands. The girl can't be a day over nineteen. Maybe twenty at the most, which legally makes the girl accountable for her actions. Caught between adolescence and adulthood, the girl is physically developed beyond her years. However, her body is a series of bad decisions, from the piercings on the eyebrows, nose, and lips, to the butterfly tattoo between her breasts; this girl doesn't take time to consider the consequences.

The young girl's sobs ricochet off of the walls; she knows more than anyone else what transpired in this room an hour ago, but shame has seized her tongue. Moments have passed and while I grow more intrigued by the young girl who sits in front of me, I am aware that my original question has not been answered. "Don't all speak at once."

Two honorable but naïve deacons search each other's blank faces for answers.

"We don't know," Deacon Townsend, the man who hired me, says. I consider Townsend my point man in this situation. He is the guy who will give me all of the information I need in order to be successful. So far, Deacon Townsend is off to a mediocre start. He knows why Pastor Lewis left, which is obvious, but Deacon Townsend doesn't know where the pastor is at the present moment.

"Pastor Lewis is probably at home with the first lady," Deacon Chambers, the other man in the room, says.

More than likely, Deacon Chambers is right. It is a Friday and Pastor Lewis's church, True Vine, has just concluded a week-long revival. It is not uncommon for a pastor to come home late from a revival. I imagine he probably longs for a chance to fellowship with his fellow colleagues as a cover. So long as he does not come home too late, Pastor Lewis has time for a rendezvous. Where the story gets a little muddled is why Pastor Lewis got a hotel room in downtown Detroit? Discretion is key to an affair. This room is not discrete, which means the luxurious hotel room was the girl's idea. Something transpired here that caused Pastor Lewis to up and leave and it was not a crisis of his conscience.

The young girl's sobs reach an insufferable level, which means that she does not appreciate being neglected. There is something that is hidden that she wants us to discover, something that has to do with her face. To tell the truth I did not even look at her face.

I can only assume that my astute colleagues have not taken a look at her face either. I kneel down and gently pry the girl's hands from her face. She reveals a developing black eye. I along with the two deacons wince at the sight. Beyond the rebellious tattoos and piercings lies a little girl who now has to add "abuse victim" to her ever-expanding resume.

A room that smells like sex and hard liquor and a distraught girl with a bruise on her body is not a foreign scene for me. Frankly, I have seen this scene play out many times before which made it simple for how I would resolve this matter.

"Who is Pastor Lewis's successor?" I ask.

"Pastor Givens," Deacon Townsend replies after some hesitation.

"Contact him and congratulate him on becoming the new senior pastor of True Vine Baptist Church," I say.

"But what about Pastor Lewis?" Deacon Chambers asks.

"He's done. The second he put his hands on this young lady it became a criminal act. You might as well cut your losses and save your church."

"Well, with all due respect, Minister Dungy, you were hired to help fix this problem. Why else would we call you?" Deacon Townsend asks.

I move away from the young girl to make eye contact with Deacon Townsend. At five feet eight we are virtually the same height, but my stature dwarfs his and so I feel like I am the bigger man.

"You hired me because Pastor Lewis was having an affair and he refused to listen to any one of his elders. You hired me to keep the church from folding from a scandal and that is exactly what I am going to do. Now as far as I'm concerned when it comes to Pastor Lewis, I couldn't care less. He better hope that I leave town before I see him or he's going to have a black eye of his own."

It is sheep like Deacon Townsend who make me thankful that I am no longer a minister at a church. While I still have all the papers and certificates that confirm me to be an ordained minister, I do not belong to a particular church. I can't put my faith in people. I can only put my faith in God. Take for example this particular situation;

Deacon Townsend is more concern about his loyalty to Pastor Lewis than his loyalty to the Gospel.

"Sweetheart, I'm going to take you to the hospital. Do you have medical insurance?" I ask her. The girl shakes her head no. I stand up and make eye contact with Deacon Townsend. "Don't worry," I say to the girl without taking my eyes off of Deacon Townsend. "The church will take care of your hospital bill."

"Minister Dungy!" Deacon Townsend interjects, but I put up my hand to stop him. I gesture for us to step outside.

Deacon Townsend adheres to my request and follows me outside the door. "Minister Dungy, I thought—"

"Not here," I say and I continue to walk down the hall toward the elevator. The hallway kind of reminds me of the Overlook Hotel from the book *The Shining*. Just the thought of what happened in that story gives me an eerie feeling. Of course I always have an unpleasant feeling whenever I am in an antiquated hotel.

It doesn't come as a surprise that Deacon Townsend doesn't hesitate to follow me to the elevator; being a follower seems indicative of his character. We share a moment as we wait for the elevator to arrive and admire our reflections in the elevator doors. We have striking resemblances until the door splits our images open and we enter the elevator. Even in the elevator Deacon Townsend resists the temptation to say anything. He is loyal to his master and does not want this scandal to be leaked as a result of his inability to use discretion.

We get off the elevator and make our way through a well-lit lobby, which I presume has not had any renovations since the sixties. Of course classic hotels have the luxury of remaining luxurious through the years. We don't say a word to each other as we leave the hotel and walk across the street to where my rental car is parked.

To Deacon Townsend's disappointment I did not call him outside to convey some secret advice that I did not want anyone within earshot to hear; no, instead I asked Townsend to follow me outside so that I can take in the icy Detroit air and for me to indulge in one of my many vices. I reach into the inside pocket of my wool sports coat and remove a cigarette. I light the cigarette and take a drag and exhale the smoke into the merciless cold air.

I appreciate the cold that the Motor City has to offer, especially coming from a place where sixty-degree weather meant that we'd entered winter. It is the cold of Detroit that breeds men of steel, which is why most cities have folded due to the economic depravity, but the Motor City remains resolute and keeps right on moving.

"Minister Dungy, I don't understand how this works," Deacon Townsend says.

"I'm going to tell you exactly how this is going to work. Your church is seventy percent women, about twenty percent men, and the rest are made up of children. A pastor having an adulterous affair is one thing, but a pastor being arrested for physically assaulting a woman is an entirely different thing all together. You will lose the bulk of your women, which means that you will lose their husbands and children as well." I tap Deacon Townsend on the head as a gesture for him to think. One of my biggest pet peeves is when I have to talk to grown men like they're five-year-olds. To me this situation is real simple: cut Pastor Lewis like a pound cake and move on.

I take another drag of my cigarette because I believe that for the first time Deacon Townsend comprehends the ramifications of his Pastor Lewis's actions. "If you want to get ahead of this thing then you will get Pastor Lewis to resign as senior pastor of True Vine. Put in a new pastor with a different vision and get Pastor Lewis the help that he needs: anger management, marital counseling, whatever, but get him help.

"If the media or people start asking questions you can say that you are against Pastor Lewis's actions. You've gotten help for both the pastor and the young lady and you plan to make a generous donation to a shelter for battered women. If you do that then you will save your church. If not, well, what do I care? I have already cashed the check." I release a trail of smoke from my mouth.

"Pastor Lewis is an anointed man of God. He is an honorable man," Townsend says.

"I don't know if Pastor Lewis is a good man, Deacon, but I believe you are. Pastor Lewis is going to need men like you to help him get back on track."

"I can't thank you enough for all of your help," Townsend says.

"You already thanked me when you paid me. You're a good guy, Deacon, and I know you want to help, so I trust that you will do the best for your congregation and for the Gospel."

"It was a pleasure working with you." Deacon Townsend extends his hand and I give him a firm shake.

"It shouldn't be. Now go and produce the girl. I'll take her to the hospital."

The deacon does not hesitate to go inside and get the girl. While I wait for the girl to come down I look into the sky. I don't look for stars in a smog-filled sky. I look for God and understanding of why I have been cursed with this gift to solve problems.

The girl comes out in the cold. She has on a different outfit, but it hardly qualifies as an improvement. Her attire further proves the point that she is a confused little girl in a black leather skirt. Deacon Townsend covers her with his sport coat and bears the weather.

"We're going to the hospital, princess," I say before I open the door.

The girl gets into the car and I finish my cigarette in time to flick it off into the night. I give Deacon Townsend a head nod as I walk around to the driver side. I get into the car and the girl's sobs have decreased dramatically. I turn on the ignition, and wait for the car to warm up before I drive off.

I remember where Pastor Lewis lives. I have half a mind to show up at his house and present the battered girl as a trophy to his wife. Instead I remain professional and exit the hotel parking lot, heading for the hospital. Deacon Townsend is still outside in the cold when I leave, just like a good dog.

Rather than listen to the girl sob, I turn on the radio and channel surf until I arrived at Marvin Gaye's "Inner City Blues." My windshield did its best to combat the snow falling from the sky, and at the first light I reach into my pocket for another cigarette. I fire up and by the time the light turns green, I take another drag.

"Excuse me." I let down the window long enough to let the cigarette smoke escape out of the window.

"I've never met a minister who smokes," the girl says.

"I'm honored."

The girl winces from the sting of her bruised eye. I never know what to say in situations like this where I'm driving a broken woman home or to the hospital in this manner. To be honest, my thoughts are consumed by my work, and when I will have seen enough to walk away.

"Everything is going to be okay," I say to the girl.

"I stopped believing that a long time ago."

I do not know how to follow that response. She is not my client and it is counterproductive to get to know her. Those are the only words spoken until we arrive at the county hospital. I pull around to the back of the hospital where the emergency room entrance is located. I stop at the stop sign with no intentions to park or go inside.

"What am I supposed to tell them?" the girl asks.

"The truth. Pastor Lewis won't hurt you anymore. When you get your bill, give it to the church and they will take care of it."

"Then what?"

"Then you go home or you sue Pastor Lewis; I don't know, princess. What I do know is that you don't go after True Vine. Whenever you get the opportunity you commend True Vine for how they handled the situation."

The girl steps back from the car and is about to walk away until I motion for her to stop. "God hasn't abandoned you. I know it seems like that, but He hasn't. God still has a plan for you."

"Whatever," the girl says as she steps away from the car. I watch her enter through the sliding glass doors before I pull away. I have two hours before my flight leaves. Two hours is a lot of time. It is enough time for me to make a quick stop.

As a kid I always wanted to live in a mansion made of all bricks. I always thought that brick mansions were the best because they seemed built to withstand any storm. Pastor Lewis has a brick mansion, just like the one that I dreamt about when I was a kid. Somehow I feel like Pastor Lewis's house will not survive the storm that is heading his way.

I flick my cigarette into the night and roll up my window as I exit the car. I walk up the driveway of the Lewis residence and ring the doorbell. Even in an affluent neighborhood, the pressures of the recession have caused certain homeowners to add extra security measures. Pastor Lewis has a front gate that begins at the edge of the driveway, and bars on the windows. I can tell that the bars and gate have recently been added because there isn't any rust or chipped paint.

"My goodness, Minister Dungy, it's late," First Lady Lewis says. She emerges from the door in her pink nightgown and robe. First Lady even has her hair wrapped, and given my experience with black women I know that she does not want me to see her in her nightgown, hair net, and rollers.

"I'm terribly sorry, First Lady Lewis, to bother you at this hour. I really need to speak with Pastor Lewis."

"I'm sorry, but it's late and he just got back from a meeting."

Yeah, he just got back from a meeting, but not the kind you would approve of. "I know, but I'm about to get on a plane and go and I need to just talk with him."

First Lady gives me a grin and unlocks the gate. I step into the space between the gate and the front door.

"Be quick about it. He's in his study. I'll show you the way," First Lady Lewis says.

"Thank you so much."

I follow First Lady into the house and embrace the warmth courtesy of the central heater. We walk past the staircase to a door behind the staircase. First Lady gives a polite knock on the door.

"The door is closed for a reason!" a voice says from the other side of the door.

"I know, but Minister Dungy is here. He needs to see you before he leaves," First Lady Lewis says.

Pastor Lewis doesn't say anything. I can only imagine what is going through Pastor Lewis's mind. In truth I could've let the whole incident go. I have my money, the church has an exit strategy, the girl is at the hospital, and the church will pick up the tab. But my father used my mother and I as punching bags until I got older, and for that alone I can't let it go.

The door opens wide enough for me to see Pastor Lewis's pig nose. Pastor Lewis then opens the door all the way to let me in.

"Could I get you guys anything?" First Lady Lewis asks.

"We're fine!" Pastor Lewis speaks for both of us as he slams the door shut and locks it.

It takes me a moment to position myself while Pastor Lewis's back is turned. As soon as Pastor Lewis turns around I cock back my right hand and fire right to his pig nose. I feel the sting of my hand that suggests I will be in a lot of pain later, but for now it feels good. While Pastor Lewis holds his nose and says muffled curse words at me, I use the time to locate the stereo on his desk. Over the last week I have become familiar with Pastor Lewis's office. I turn on the stereo and James Cleveland bursts through the speakers, which allows for me and the not-so-good pastor to talk.

Pastor Lewis manages to recover from the blow and makes his way toward me. His body is exposed and he has made the mistake of mistaking me for a nineteen-year-old girl. Pastor Lewis swings with an overhand right and I block his punch and counter with a hard punch to the sternum. Pastor Lewis falls down to one knee and gasps for air.

I kneel down in front of Pastor Lewis. "I had to drop a young girl off at the emergency room. Tell me why I had to drop a girl off at the emergency room?"

"You don't understand." Pastor Lewis winces as he speaks.

"Explain to me how your meeting to end the affair with a nineteen-year-old ended with the girl having a black eye and other possible bruises."

"I went to break it off as you said, but she had on this lingerie and I couldn't resist."

The one thing I hate worst than liars are pastors who lie. "I specifically told you not to meet with her without me and certainly not at some hotel!"

"She tricked me, man. The devil has corrupted her. She threatened to tell my wife, to confront me in front of the congregation. I lost it, man! I lost it for a split second." Lewis looks up at the ceiling. "Oh, Father, forgive me! Lord, I don't want to go jail or lose my family."

I get up and walk away from Pastor Lewis. At this point I can't stand the sight of him. I take a seat on Pastor Lewis's desk and look at the pictures of Pastor Lewis and his wife and three children: Aaron, Janice, and Benjamin. For as long as I shall live, I won't understand what makes a man give away his treasure for trash.

"What happened to you?" My question breaks the chorus of Pastor Lewis's sobs. "You used to walk in so much anointing and power that I thought you would be like the prophet Elijah and walk right into heaven. But now . . . now you're down here on earth with the rest of us. I never expected to get a call from you. Never in a million years did I think that the mighty Pastor Lewis would need my help."

"Minister Dungy, you got to help me."

"I tried to help you, but I can't. It's done; the church is going to remove you as senior pastor. There's nothing more I can do."

"There's something that can be done. Please don't let them take my church away from me."

"No man is bigger than his church. You did this to yourself, and if I were you, I would be more concerned about losing my family. That's what's really important."

That is the one thing I've learned over the years, that a title means nothing if your family isn't in your corner.

"Will you pray with me? Please!" Pastor Lewis is still on his knees begging. It's a pathetic sight.

At one point Pastor Lewis commanded a church that has over 10,000 members. He now sits on his knees in need of prayer, a need that I can't fulfill. I know that God has forgiven Pastor Lewis, but I haven't and I don't plan to anytime soon.

"Please!" Pastor Lewis says again.

I get up and walk over to Pastor Lewis. I put my hand on his shoulder and say a silent prayer before I head out the door. I leave Pastor Lewis in his office to sob while James Cleveland plays on his stereo. I cannot spend any more time in Detroit. I have a plane to catch and a job to do.

Chapter Two

I am a man without a church, a minister without a pulpit. I hold no official title at any denomination and that means I answer to no one but God. I am also a man of principle. Sometimes my principles exist in a gray area, but I am a man of principle nonetheless. One of my standards is that I fly first class no matter where I go. Since I spend the majority of my time in the air, I make sure that I am comfortable. Sometimes even when I have the best seat in the house, peace and comfort are elusive.

As I struggle to adjust my seat, I am anything but comfortable. I should've never lowered my standards and allowed my next job to convince me to fly coach. After all, I was doing this church a favor by coming out; a first-class flight is not an unreasonable request.

From Detroit I head to Houston, Texas. It is a detour from my next stop, but an old friend calls in for a big favor. My friend promises that the job will require no more than a few hours of my time. I have a firm rule that I don't go anywhere unless my travel has been taken care of and that half of my fee has been paid. My friend went through great lengths to come up with half of my fee and my plane ticket, and his friendship is worth the detour. My body has to switch from the Eastern Time Zone to the Central Time Zone. I find a position in my seat that is somewhat comfortable and close my eyes.

The battered girl is at the forefront of my mind. A pastor who will go so far as to put his hands on a woman is not a shepherd but a wolf. I don't make follow-up calls to see how things turn out, but I wonder about the girl and what will become of her life.

The flight attendant comes by and I order a drink. After a few drinks, my nerves settle. I can't sleep but what else is new? My job as an independent problem solver is emotionally taxing. I close my eyes because the most I can do is rest my eyes.

In the morning, the plane has taxied to the runway. The seatbelt sign goes off and I get up without hesitation. I need to stretch because my back feels stiff, one of the benefits of middle age. The one thing I love about flying is that when I am 30,000 feet in the air, my cell phone doesn't ring. The one thing I hate about flying is that my body always stiffens up during the course of the flight.

I grab my bags and I am held up by the passengers in front of me. *What is with people who take all day to grab their things and leave?* I wish I could leap over them and walk out the door.

People start to exit the plane and I make my way through the Houston Intercontinental Airport. I haven't shaved in a week and that is apparent, but my unshaved appearance is offset by my Italian-cut gray suit and white collar shirt. I am a firm believer in wearing a nice suit to work. I am more exhausted than hungry, but I won't stop to rest nor eat, not until the job is done.

Outside at the arrival section of the airport, a Lincoln Town Car with the words MOUNT ZION BAPTIST CHURCH on the side door pulls in along the curb. My friend and point man, Deacon Thomas Burt, gets out of the driver side and jogs around the front of the car.

"It's been a long time, Nic." Burt extends his hand.

"Too long, and I wish it were for better circumstances." I shake Burt's hand.

Burt offers to handle my bags, which I decline. I throw my bag in the back seat and keep my briefcase with me as I get into the front seat. We pull away from the parking lot, making our way to Mount Zion.

"You know I don't normally do this," I say.

"I know, but I need your help. Pastor is going to wreck his life if you don't step in."

"You're his closest friend. If he's not going to listen to you, then I doubt there's much more I can do."

"You have a skill set that I believe will be persuasive." Burt picks up the speed of the Town Car.

My skill set is the secret to my success, but my key to employment is that I can do something that most ministerial staff and congregations can't do: I hold the leaders accountable. I get the leaders help and I minimize a potentially disastrous situation, but I also make sure that the leaders know that I will not be around the next time they blow it.

"Are you sure it's there?" I ask.

"I wish it weren't, but it is."

"Okay, well, I'm going to need a key to his office."

"I got you." Burt doesn't take his eyes off the road.

I go into my briefcase and pull out my laptop. I power on my laptop and connect the wireless device so that I can go online. Once my computer is up I go to YouTube and I type in Pastor Jeremiah Surges. Pastor is quite popular on YouTube since he has a lot of his sermons posted on it.

"Give me the dates again," I say.

"I don't remember the dates. I just remember the titles. One was 'I got to get myself together.'"

I scroll through the sermons and locate I Got to Get Myself Together. I start to view the footage.

"Do you see it?" Burt asks me.

It takes a moment for me to process what I am seeing. "I see."

"Go to 'I can't come down,'" Burt says.

I pull up that video and that image is even more obvious than the previous video. I have more than enough information and I just need to meet with the man face to face.

Pastor Jeremiah Surgess sways from side to side and takes a moment to hold on to the podium. His mannerism is awkward even for a preacher who likes to whoop and holler.

"Yes!" Surgess says with sweat pouring down his face profusely. It doesn't matter though; the church is a sweat box. Even in the first week of November, I can see water on the walls. Only the ceiling fans provide some relief to the sanctuary. No, Pastor Surgess's sweat is not a tell-tale sign.

"You see the apostle Peter had a thorn in his flesh. We got it wrong; we think that God put it there, but it was the devil. God gave him the grace and power to overcome the thorn in his flesh. Just like He gave you the grace to overcome the thorns in your life."

The congregation responds in a fever pitch. Few notice that Surgess cites Apostle Peter instead of Apostle Paul. I am impressed with Pastor Surgess and his sermon and I understand how his sermons can mesmerize a congregation. Pastor Surgess is so robust with a hump in his back and it adds flair to his delivery. He leans forward and holds on to the podium to keep his balance. I take out my mini camera from my briefcase and I begin to record.

"Only authorized personal can record," an usher says a few minutes later.

"I'm sorry, this is just really powerful. I'll put my camera away." I do as the usher asked and I put my camera away. I have more than enough footage.

By the time I put my camera away, Pastor Surgess has taken a break on the steps of the podium to catch his breath.

"Hey, hey, hey!" is Pastor Surgess's signature phrase he shouts, which is what most pastors are famous for now. That phrase is also an indication that Surgess's message is near a close.

I have heard and seen enough and with the final slur of speech, I make my way out of the sanctuary. As I walk through the lobby my contact person, Deacon Burt, hands me the keys to Pastor Surgess's office. I take the keys without eye contact or breaking stride. I enter the office and embraced the cool central air. My suit is practically stuck to me as a result of the heat.

I go into my briefcase and remove my laptop, my mini camera, and plastic gloves. I can't afford to leave any evidence that I was here. After I put on my gloves, I turn on my laptop and use a USB cord to link my camera and my laptop. I upload the footage from the service and add to my profile. While my computer compiles all of my evidence, I then search for the missing piece to the puzzle.

I make my way to the bookshelf behind Pastor Surgess's leather chair. I look behind a row of books stacked in a nice column. I remove a few books and in the corner is a bottle of cognac.

The bottle is not well hidden, but who will guess that a bottle of cognac will be hidden in the corner of a pastor's bookshelf? There is no way I can preach with alcohol in my system, but Surgess can and he has for a number of years until his best friend Deacon Burt's conscience kicked in. I take a couple of pictures from my camera phone before I remove the bottle from the shelf and twist the cap of the bottle.

The smell from the cognac causes my mouth to water, and if it weren't for more pressing issues, I would take a glass of this fine brandy. Instead I set the bottle down on the desk and I take a seat in the leather chair.

Thirty minutes later, Pastor Surgess enters the office and in a matter of seconds his expression goes from shock to anger to shame when I point to the bottle of cognac.

"I've got to hand it to you. I've heard a lot of drunken preachers, but most of them are outside of a liquor store. You're one of the first I know who can preach from the actual pulpit."

"I don't know what you're talking about," Pastor Surgess responds.

"Denial. That's a step that you'll have to work on and you will. I'm here by way of your best friend, Deacon Burt, who is worried about your ministry."

"I'm not!" Pastor Surgess snaps.

"You were elected into your ministry by a board. They find out that you like to preach while inebriated and it's over."

"I'm not stepping down!"

"I'm not talking about stepping down, just stepping aside." I reach into my jacket and hand him a packet of info to a recovery program with a plane ticket included. "Take time to get help."

"I don't need any help. I got the grace of God."

"God's grace is not a license for you to sin. Your best friend is an honorable man, but when he came to you, you put your hands around his throat."

"If I didn't listen to my best friend then what makes you think that I would listen to you?'

I stand up and turn my laptop around to show all of the footage and documentation. I have a collection that supports my claim. Deacon Burt provided me with footage from previous sermons and events where Pastor Surgess behavior was questionable. I remove from my briefcase documentation of DUIs from the past when Pastor Surgess

was just starting out in ministry. I managed to print out
the documents from Surgess's printer while I waited for
Surgess to show up.

"Deacon Burt loves you too much to do this, but I don't.
This information along with video footage would not
only go viral, but it will find itself in the inbox of other
board members if you don't go into the program. There's
a recovery center in Alabama that I'm sending you to;
it's one of the best. Deacon Burt will tell the other board
members that you went on leave. If you choose not to go,
well, I'm sure Minister Weiss, who has been eyeing your
position for a while, will love for this information to see
the light of day."

"So what's to stop me from kicking your tail?"

I close my laptop and put away all of my things into my
briefcase. I walk up to Pastor Surgess with my briefcase
in hand. "For one, you know this is the right thing. And
for two, you can't!"

I move past Pastor Surgess, not intimidated by his
empty threat as I head toward the door.

"You know I heard about you?" Pastor Surgess says
and his words stop me dead in my tracks. "You fashion
yourself as a minister but you and I both know you're a
wolf in sheep's clothing."

Maybe he is right, maybe I am a wolf, but I would
rather be a paid wolf than a penniless sheep. "Do the right
thing, Pastor Surgess."

I shrugged off Pastor Surgess's comment and walk
away from the office with a smile on my face because my
business in Houston has concluded. Now I have just one
more stop before I head home.

Chapter Three

In West Virginia the snow falls like ash from the sky. I thought Detroit was cold, but West Virginia looks like a blizzard has taken permanent residence here.

"Thank goodness your heater is working," I say.

"Yes, sir. You're used to sunny California, where the weather don't know what it wants to do these days. Our weather has its mind made up," Mr. Willard says.

We drive along a road that has endless trees and few neighborhoods in-between. There is one conclusion I draw as I ride along and listen to Clint Black: the people who live out here pay for seclusion.

"Listen, I better not be in danger and those things better be put away."

"Don't worry; he doesn't keep them in the house. He has a caretaker," Mr. Willard says.

Mr. Willard is the church's attorney. Given the uniqueness of the services this church provides, I will say that having a lawyer on retainer is a smart move. West Virginia is a drastic change from the cold that Detroit bought and the warmth that Houston brought. West Virginia brings a picturesque setting with tall trees covered in snow; it feels like Christmas has already arrived. The snow is as white as Mr. Willard's hair. I feel small as the minivan whips around on a two-lane highway.

We continue down this one road and I wonder which is faster: the plane ride or the ride in the car. Right now, the plane ride was relaxing and this car ride is never-ending.

I know I am going into the rural part of West Virginia, but this is absurd.

This next case is ripped from a horror movie and even though my instincts tell me to stay away from this case, my greed speaks louder. Finally we turn off the road and towering trees that resemble Greek columns lead to a white mansion. The mansion is surrounded by a gate that needs to be fixed, but it still works. My contact, Mr. Willard, pulls up to the intercom.

"Praise the Lord and welcome," I hear a voice from the intercom.

"It's Mr. Willard with our guest," Mr. Willard says.

I roll my eyes at the over-the-top greeting. The gate opens and Mr. Willard drives around the full-circle gravel driveway to the front door. A family of three walks out of the house. The wife is wearing a white dress that is brighter than her skin. The son is decked out in a white suit, and the husband, Reverend Mac Swagger, has on white slacks, and a white collar shirt minus the tie. I can see the angle this family is trying to portray.

"God bless you, Minister Dungy." Reverend Swagger shakes my hand. "This is my wife, Martha, and my son, Ezekiel."

"How do you do?" Martha asks.

"Good afternoon and God bless," I say before I shake the wife's and son's hands.

"I'm so blessed that both parties agreed to meet here. I'm having Rosa whip up something special for lunch."

I hate the rich because they think that their level of comfort can cover up the most egregious actions. For a moment we stand outside in the cold for no good earthly reason and I forget the reason I am here until another car pulls up to the gate. I am surprised that this Mercury Sable survives the trip; its noise of a failing engine precedes the car's arrival.

"Rosa! Our other guests are here!" Reverend Swagger says.

Moments later the car rolls through the gate and stops just behind the minivan. I remember my reason for being at the Swagger residence when a woman and her preteen child emerge. The boy has his arm in a sling and the mother has on a sundress with black stockings that do nothing to define her figure, and a thick wool coat that is an even greater fashion offense.

I turn back to look at Reverend Swagger. His "Praise the Lord" smile has disappeared and he now has a look of disdain.

"Hello, Meredith," Martha says. The two women have met before.

Reverend Swagger insisted that all involved parties meet at his home. Swagger, I figure, wants the home-court advantage, but for now Meredith and her son, Joel, have the emotional advantage. There are serial combustible elements at work here and this situation can easily get out of hand.

"Well, let's go inside, shall we, before we freeze to death?" Mr. Willard makes a gesture for all parties to go inside.

I trail behind the boy as the rest of the group walks into the house. This house must've been designed for a giant because it is ten feet high; when I walk inside there is a chandelier that is big enough and bright enough to light up Vegas. Martha takes Ezekiel upstairs and we enter the living room that is designed for a pharaoh. Gold-rimmed coffee tables and expensive vases; Reverend Swagger makes a killing as a preacher.

"Please have a seat," Reverend Swagger says.

We all sit on the ultra-plush couch and I feel my five foot eight inch frame as it sinks into the couch. Once I have established some level of comfort, I notice the eighty-inch plasma TV on Swagger's wall. Meredith helps Joel onto the couch and I don't know if I should've helped or remained on the couch. After all, Reverend is the client.

"So should we discuss why we're here?" Mr. Willard asks.

I hold up my hand. "Actually, thank you, Mr. Willard, this is the part where I come in. But before we get started, since we are here in the spirit of doing things according to God's will, let us pray."

Reverend Swagger is reluctant but he takes Ms. Lancing by the hands. I take the young boy's hand and Mr. Willard completes the link.

"Heavenly Father, we gather here to seek wisdom and comfort in this difficult time. Lord, we know that your Word does not want disputes among Christians to be settled in the courts. So I ask in Jesus' name that we have an open mind and an open heart. In Jesus' name we pray. Amen." I conclude my prayer and the parties don't waste any time loosening their grips.

I get up and go into my briefcase and remove a CD. I make my way over to the entertainment center and after a few moments of fumbling around I manage to get both the TV and the DVD player to work. I stand next to the TV like a driver's education instructor and wait for the movie to come on.

A video comes on with Reverend Swagger in an outfit identical to the one he has on today. "Praise the Lord and praise the courageous faithful," Swagger says.

The video seems like a normal church service, except Reverend Swagger has two rattle snakes in his hands. Snake handling is outlawed in most states except for West Virginia, Kentucky, and a few other Southern states.

I find it hard to imagine that in an age when there is a black president, cell phones that can play movies, and maps that talk to you, there are still people who believe in foolish traditions like snake handling. I wait until I have everyone's attention before I stop the video.

"On October fourth of this year Meredith and Joel Lancing attended your snake handling service, during which twelve-year-old Joel was bitten by a snake and had to be rushed to the hospital. We're here today to settle this matter without the involvement of the courts and the media."

I take a look at Reverend Swagger and his face is flushed as he rubs his lips. Meredith comforts her son as if the mere image of the snake causes her to relive the episode all over.

"I want you to pay for what you did to my son." Meredith words are full of vile and disdain toward Reverend Swagger.

"The Word clearly declares in Matthew 17 that if you have faith, you can trend upon serpents. It breaks my heart what happened to your boy, but that's because he lacks faith."

I want to backhand Reverend Swagger for his backward thinking, but $25,000 is my fee and that is more than enough reason to give me pause. "Look, the point is that no one wants to drag this out in court, which is why I have Mr. Willard here to notarize an agreement between two parties."

"I want $200,000," Meredith says.

Reverend Swagger lets out a curse word and does not bother to apologize.

"You're going to burn in hell. I've racked up twenty thousand in medical bills."

$20,000 for a snake bite might be an exaggeration, but then again nothing is out of bounds when it comes to health care.

"Hold on! Now let's put the emotion aside and work things out," I say.

"I refuse to pay $200,000 for doing the Lord's will," Reverend Swagger says.

"Well, how much are you willing to pay?" I ask.

Reverend Swagger picks up a notepad that is on the coffee table. He pulls out his gold ballpoint pen and starts writing. He takes the note and folds it before he hands the note to me. I open the note and read the figure: $10,000. I hold back the smirk. This man is incredible.

"Can you do math?" I ask Reverend Swagger and the question was rhetorical. "Multiply that number by five."

"Fifty thousand dollars!" Reverend Swagger is floored by my counter offer.

"That's it!" Meredith says.

"That's a fair deal. Mrs. Lancing, you went to this church willingly, and judging by your economic situation a good defense lawyer can make a case that you were looking for a payday. The last thing you need is to rack up a legal bill on top of your medical bills."

I turn to Reverend Swagger. "And, Reverend Swagger, seriously? Your ministry brings in two million a year; fifty thousand is a parking ticket."

Reverend Swagger sits back in his couch and rubs his face. "Okay, done!"

"And a new car!" Meredith says.

"I actually agree with that," I say. Meredith's car is an embarrassment.

Reverend Swagger rubs his face and nods his head in agreement. Mr. Willard types up the agreement on his laptop and prints it from Reverend Swagger's office. Both parties sign and my work in Virginia is done.

In retrospect, I could've gotten Meredith to accept the $10,000 without a new car, but sometimes I like sticking it to the wealthy loony tunes.

Chapter Four

I love red-eye flights. Give me a plane filled with exhausted businessmen, grieving family members, and a few children and I am a happy passenger. I prefer a somber plane ride as opposed to a vibrant one with people who are on their way to Disneyland or whatever vacation spot they have lined up. On a red-eye flight, we are all on the same accord; we are all trying to get to our destination with minimal annoyance.

Most of the passengers are in their second REM cycle of sleep, which means a drop in cabin pressure or a little turbulence is unlikely to wake them up. Otherwise the rest of the plane settles into a night of uncomfortable sleep. The workaholics punch away on their laptops. I stare out of the window in awe of how far our aviation program has come. We float above the clouds in the cloak of night. I have plenty of leg room and for the first time this trip I find comfort.

While the plane cruises above 30,000 feet I often think about plane crashes. I know it's morbid to think about plane crashes while on a plane, but I can't help but to think about what went through the minds of the plane crash victims right before the crash. Did they have plans for when the plane landed? Of course. Did they feel like they had all the time in the world? When reality hit them that this could be the end, were there regrets on how they spent their time? Did they think about God and what awaited them in the afterlife? In my case, I would have regrets and wish that my life would've gone in a different direction.

To be fair, for the last year I started to question whether I still had the temperament to be a church problem solver. The job itself is taxing both spiritually and mentally. I created a job out of an infrastructure that is supposed to only have one problem solver: Jesus Christ. I often wonder after I finish a job if in fact it is my last job, and I will retire from the problem-solving business. Maybe God has a different profession for me. Maybe I can go back to school and complete my doctoral work in sociology. I even considered a career in real estate; I am sure that the market is bound to recover. I believe if anyone would understand my plight it would be God. He would understand why I've grown weary working with His people.

"Are you reading that?" the woman in the seat next to me asks, but I am not sure what she is talking about until I turn toward her and look down to where she points. She points at the magazine that sits on top of my tray table. The latest copy of *Gospel Magazine Today* has Bishop Wade of Everlasting Christian Center. Bishop Wade is on the rise and his church averages at least a hundred new members per week.

"No, no, I wasn't. Go ahead."

The woman takes the magazine before I can reach a period on my sentence. "I just love him. He has such a great anointing," she says from her chocolate lips.

"Yes, he does," I say while mentally I recall a call from Bishop Wade's wife years ago. She needed me to come in and help with Bishop Wade's closet homosexuality problem. A member of his congregation was ready to come forth and expose Bishop Wade. It was nothing more than a greedy person who wanted a quick payday, so we paid him hush money and Bishop Wade sought counseling and help.

Wade went on hiatus, and if it were not for me and the love and devotion of his wife and, of course, God, Bishop Wade certainly would not be on the cover of *Gospel Magazine Today.*

"So what do you do?" the woman asks.

"I'm in the PR profession," I say, which is not a lie. I am in the PR profession, but that does not stand for public relations. My employers tend to have me deal in private relations. They pay a great deal of money to have me resolve their issues and they pay me even more for my silence.

"My firm could use you," the woman says with a smile.

"What type of law do you practice?"

The question catches the woman off-guard. Rather than ask me how I know she is a lawyer, the woman does a quick scan to see if she left any evidence. The woman has legal briefs on top of her tray table. The notes scribbled on her yellow legal pad are all tell-tale signs, but I look deeper than that. The woman has to be in her early forties but if someone had to guess her age most men would say thirty-five at best.

She has a manicure that can't be more than two days old. Her hair is styled and she has impeccable posture, which means that she gives off an aura of strength.

"Business law. I don't even want to think about the day I will have in the morning." She lies back and rests her head against the seat.

"You'll do fine; just remember who you serve." I can't help but to smile.

"Ain't that the truth? So what church do you go to?"

"I don't belong to a particular church, but I do go as much as I can. God knows my heart."

"He does and that's all that matters."

***

Now for someone who travels on the road as much as I do, it is difficult to call one place home. I have an apartment in Carson, California to store my clothes and receive mail. Nestled between Compton and North Long Beach, Carson is a city filled with predominantly working-class African Americans who desire a safer neighborhood and the house of their dreams. I love the area, but with the expansion of businesses and the construction of the Home Depot Center, even this once-familiar city is starting to become foreign to me.

I am grateful when the plane touches down at Los Angeles International Airport. LAX on a day like today is perfect for film crews.

After going from one extreme weather condition to the next, it's nice to be back home where the wind has a subtle presence and the sun has held back the brunt of its force as 747 planes both depart and touch down. I taxi my way to the long-term parking lot to pick my midnight blue BMW 325. In retrospect, I bought the car to have some semblance of my success. The problem-solving business has brought forth serious monetary gains. But the car has been subject to constant neglect by my hands. I hardly wash it, hardly keep up with the maintenance of it, and the smell of leather has long succumbed to the smell of menthol.

Without traffic on the 405, which is rare, I get from the airport to Carson inside of fifteen minutes. It's a beautiful drive and right now the jazz radio station is playing such a great collection of music that it makes me want to stay on this freeway until I reach San Diego, but I am hungry and I can't ignore my appetite.

At R & R Soul Food I decide to indulge in some grits and eggs with wheat toast and coffee. I find peace in the quaint restaurant that is adjacent to the Home Depot Center. Ten years ago that area was all unused land that sat on the grounds of Cal State Dominguez, but it is nice to see that despite the city's growth, most of the restaurants here have been around through the decades. I find solitude as I read the sports section of the *Daily Breeze*. My life is full of turmoil. I have no interest to read anyone else's turmoil that finds its way on the front page.

"Nicodemus Dungy, the living legend." Paul Wallace, an old college friend and reporter for the *L.A. Times,* approaches my table and takes a seat.

"What's up, P?" We exchange fist bumps.

Like the majority of college students, I floated back and forth between majors before I settled down on one. I took journalism classes and public relations classes. I thought about a career as a criminal defense attorney, so I took criminal justice classes until I became fascinated with the function of society and people and decided to follow sociology. Paul was one of the friends I befriended while writing for the school newspaper.

"You tell me." Paul signals for a waitress to come over. "Coffee please, black with sugar," Paul says as the waitress goes away.

I know that this will not be a short visit. Even though Paul and I are close, he often plays devil's advocate and our friendship reminds me of a bad marriage. We love each other, but we can't stand each other.

"So how is the dinosaur?" I ask, which I know is a low blow. Paul desperately clings to his job, which has become a relic of the past. The printed word cannot compete with a twenty-four-hour news cycle. What is the point of reading about something that is considered old news by the time it is printed?

"How's the cloak and dagger business?" Paul shoots back.

"I don't know what you're talking about." I take a bite of my eggs.

"Seriously? You're going to play that game?' Paul says.

"You're going to ruin my breakfast?" I ask.

"Maybe, depending on how you answer this next question." Paul does not wait for me to respond before he speaks again. "How was Detroit?"

"I don't know what you're talking about," I say before I stuff more eggs into my mouth. My clients pay for both my skills and my silence; I can't afford to betray either of them. I am curious to know how Paul comes up with this information so fast. He knows my job and does not hold back in displaying his disapproval.

"You weren't in the Motor City recently?" Paul says.

"I don't know what you're talking about."

"Of course you don't. You're sworn to secrecy. I know former CIA operatives who are more forthcoming."

Paul is more agitated than usual. I can read people better than anyone and I can tell that my friend knows something that pertains directly to me.

"I'm a travelling evangelist."

"Yeah, that's funny, because I can't recall ever seeing you on TV. In fact, I don't know too many ministers who can out-drink me on a Tuesday night."

"Look, why are you busting my chops? I'm trying to have a relaxing breakfast."

"Why are you being obtuse? You're lucky that you're my only friend; otherwise, I would light you up right now."

I can tell that Paul is irritated about something. I hate the fact that Paul knows something that I don't know; and only Paul is sharp enough to beat me to a story. I am glad that he is my friend and not my enemy.

"Look, I don't know what kind of so-called ministry you do, but I know it's not God's will. Now I'll be first to tell you that I haven't been to Sunday School in quite some time."

"I would hope so. Sunday School is not for adults," I say before I take a sip of my coffee.

"Don't get cute." Paul points his finger at me, which means that he is really upset. "As I was saying, I may not be a model Christian, but I know what you're doing is wrong. If you were truly a warrior of light you wouldn't look in the shape that you are in."

My brain starts to spin out of control. *Something went wrong with one of my clients and Paul knows.* I don't know which but I know my business has been compromised.

"Look, Paul, I ain't got time for this. There's a reason why you're here so tell me what it is and let's be done with it!"

"Well, it's a darn shame what happened," Paul says with a look of disgust.

"What happened?"

"They found a pastor in his home. He shot himself."

The news steals the air in my lungs and causes me to cough. I can't believe what Paul has just said.

"What?" I ask.

"Pastor Lewis shot himself!"

The words flash on and off in my head like a neon sign and I am stuck without a word to say. I have lost my first client.

Chapter Five

I never attempt to drink cognac straight, but today is as good as any to try new things. The day hasn't even cracked the noon hour and here I am with a drink in my hand. I often question whether what I do is God's will or not. I consider my profession to be protected under the umbrella of ministry and a branch on the tree of recovery. I often wonder if I am a minister who thinks outside of the box, or if I am a little lower than a political advisor who engages in cover-ups and smear campaigns. Every question leads me to a dead end.

"Are you going to drink it or stare at it like it's a painting?" a man about two barstools down says.

"Well, it is a work of art. Its name comes from the town of Cognac in France." I finally take a swig from the glass.

"Knowing all of that fancy stuff doesn't take away from the fact that this"— the guy holds up his drink—"is a drink and its purpose is to drown your problems."

My problem seems to float no matter how much alcohol I drink. The guy and I take drinks at the same time and slam the glass on the bar. My chest burns from the taste.

"So what problems are you drowning?" I ask.

"My job gave me my walking papers." The man stares at the glass. "Nineteen years. Job said it came down to the money that I made, too. I'm upside down on my mortgage. Now I'm drinking to avoid going home and telling my wife."

"Tough break!" I take another sip after the bartender refills my glass.

"So what are you trying to drown?"

"I lost something." The golden elixir hypnotizes me and the conversation with the guy becomes muffled. Pastor Lewis committed suicide because I encouraged his church to replace him. I have gone so far from my original intention that I don't recognize the man in the mirror.

"Hello! What did you lose?" the guy asks.

I finish the rest of my drink and slam the glass on the table. In fact, I slam the glass twice to vent my frustration. I get up and pull out my wallet. I leave a hundred dollar bill on the table for the bartender.

"For mine and his drinks." I point to the guy a few seats over. I walk over to my impromptu bar buddy and pat him on the shoulder. "Go home; your wife is your best life preserver."

"Thanks." The man holds up his drink to salute me, but I walk out the door and I do not give the guy a second thought.

In the past I have had a lot of situations that did not work out like I have hoped, but never have I encountered a situation that involves a suicide. Pastor Lewis marks the first pastor I've lost and I cannot shake the fact that I had a hand in his demise.

The next two days it is hard to decipher what is true and what is false. Any guy in my position would revel in the fact that I get voicemails and e-mails full of prospective clients who are willing to pay anywhere between $25,000 to $50,000 for my services, depending on the problem and whether I actually like the client.

The price depends on the problem. I can't help but to wonder if maybe, just maybe, with so many job offers to choose from then perhaps the church had gone horribly wrong. The church in and of itself is supposed to be a recovery center. The church is a place where people from all walks of life find salvation and redemption. I used to believe in that purpose wholeheartedly. I used to not pursue monetary gain, but that was a lifetime ago. The money drives me to continue in the problem-solving business long after I lost faith in God's people.

I have $175,238.86 in my savings account. I have $53,686.34 in my checking account and I have an additional $50,000 tied up in investments and mutual funds. I don't own a house because what's the point of owning a house when you're never at home?

I have a one-bedroom apartment in Carson right by the mall, and for $1,100 per month, I'm able to pay my rent as well as some of my other bills up to six months at a time. I can walk away from my profession and take some time off to gather my thoughts.

I can only stay in bed for so long so I decide to get out of bed and make my way into the living room. I don't know if it's an occupational hazard or what, but I love a lot of space, to the point where my living room does not have massive plants or vases or a coffee table with outdated magazines on it. I have a couch pushed up against the wall; I don't own a loveseat because I am neither in love nor am I inclined to entertain a lot of visitors. I have hardwood floors and a flat-screen TV. The TV is my worst investment. I am never home to watch TV and when I am home I only watch sports and enough news to stay informed. Otherwise, I hate most news pundits, most TV shows are melodramatic and my life is much more interesting, and I hate reality shows. This apartment is easy to manage, which is essential for a tenant who has to be able to leave at a moment's notice.

The doorbell rings and I don't even need to guess who is at my door. Only one person knows where I live. Not even members of my family know my address because they all live out of state. My sequestered life is airtight to everyone except for one person. I get up and open the door before the second ring, and lo and behold it is Garland Fisherman. Garland stands outside my door like a long-lost lover hoping to get into his true love's place.

"You look great, what is your secret?" Garland says.

"A pack a day, sleep deprivation, and a stream of church scandals."

We both shared a chuckle and then a hug. Garland represents the closest thing I have to representation or management. He is the person who encourages me to help churches with the problems that they do not want to go public. After I did a great job solving a problem that involved the church we both met and worked in, Shiloh Temple, I decided to help other churches as well. In the beginning I had the best intentions, but in the end not all churches are like Shiloh. Shiloh is a great church with good, hardworking people who live by the principles of the Bible.

In retrospect, what I love about Shiloh is that it is not superficial. The people who attend Shiloh are not interested in fashion. Most members dress in casual clothes and dresses. Shiloh does not have a massive choir that is led by a charismatic choir director. I wanted to be involved in the ministry so I enrolled in the minister's class and received great instruction from Pastor Louis Green. Garland and I both flourished in ministry there, but then I discovered that Pastor Green had a problem taking one too many tips from the offering. Instead of going public, I confronted the pastor in private and got him to make a sizeable donation to the church.

I stopped going to Shiloh, but Garland keeps in touch and he is the only person I confide in from the church.

So he brings me clients and, instead of a fee, he asks that I donated money to the youth ministry. As skeptical as I am about donating money to Pastor Green's church, I trust Garland and I keep the stream of money flowing.

"You know you really should answer your phone. I've been calling you for the last two days," Garland says. He closes the door behind him and enters my place.

"I haven't really felt like talking to anyone." I resume my position on the couch, only now I am lying prostrate on it.

"I heard about what happened in Detroit. You know that wasn't your fault."

"Oh really, so the pastor decided to shoot himself for no reason? No, the one thing he loved I took away and he couldn't live with the shame of his actions."

Garland puts his hands in his pockets and begins to pace the floor, and since there is not a loveseat he can sit on, Garland sits on the opposite side of the couch. I have one chair in the dining room and other than that, my apartment gives off the "you will not be staying long" feel. Garland is used to my setup and he makes himself comfortable.

"If you could figure out and control people's actions without violating their free will, well, then that would make you smarter than God," Garland says.

"I could've thought of a way for him to keep his job, but when I saw the look on that girl's face, all I wanted to do was make him pay," I say.

"Don't let the devil into your mind. He'll never let you have it back."

I take a moment to consider my friend's words. Garland has more wisdom than half of the ministers I've seen. Maybe I did let the devil into my thoughts and that caused me to give poor advice.

"I got a job for you," Garland says.

"Not for me. I'm out the game." I sit up to find my cigarettes. I pat my pockets and find a pack. After I allow a cigarette to sit at the edge of my lips, I make my way to my granite counter to find my lighter.

"You know you should quit smoking."

"Francis Assisi smoked," I say after I light my cigarette and take a drag.

"Yeah, but he was literally being attacked by the devil every night."

"So was I; you want to see my scars?"

"I told Minister Blackwell that you would meet with him."

"I don't know why you told him that." I once again take my seat on the couch.

"Come on, Nic, everybody has a bad day at the office."

"Does your bad day end with someone committing suicide?" I shake my head as I blow out a trail of smoke.

"This isn't some corporate job that you can just walk away from. It's a calling and God has blessed you with a gift to help people and you have to answer that call."

It amazes me how after all that Garland has seen he is still hopelessly naïve. Garland continues to grow in faith while I continue to wax cold the more I deal with God's people.

I grow more skeptical. I am not skeptical of God, but I am skeptical of His people. Only Jesus could save these people and I am convinced that maybe I am standing in the way.

"Look, you could do what you want, but I was told to give you this." Garland reaches into his pocket and pulls out a folded piece of paper. "I was told to give you a figure just in case you were a little reluctant."

I take the piece of paper from Garland and open it. When I look at the figure, I decide that it can't hurt to have a conversation with this minister.

Chapter Six

$150,000. I am sure that this is not an easy problem to solve. Before I even consider the problem, I have to consider jobs that I have had in the past that did not pay me anywhere near the amount that this job is going to pay me. I once took a job in Mississippi where the pastor there was convinced that polygamy was biblically correct so the church had not one, not two, but three first ladies. The murmurs amid the congregation started to cause speculation with the local news media so for $25,000 I disposed of the problem. It turned out that one of the first ladies was not in the United States legally and that the good citizens of Belize wanted her back. The pastor quietly resigned because the Belizean wife was by far the best looking of the wives.

In Fort Lauderdale, a pastor condemned his congregation to damnation for not paying 20 percent of their wages: 10 percent tithes, and the other 10 percent to the pastor. The pastor also had a need to take additional monies from the church. That job paid me $30,000. My last job paid me $25,000 so I can only imagine what problem would cost $150,000; and would I be willing to admit if I am in over my head and leave the money on the table?

I never left any money on the table and this would be a crazy day to choose today to do so. I also never ran into a problem with a church paying my rates, but I did have a church decline my services. Now that was an interesting scenario.

"*I don't like this at all,*" Pastor Griffin said.

"*This is an honorable man. Minister Dungy is here to help,*" Pastor Jones, my contact, said.

Pastor Griffin was prideful, pig-headed, and stubborn, and those were his good qualities. He was also a violent man with a temper. His wife's lover felt the wrath of that temper and now with pending charges and a threat to do a tell-all book, here I was.

"*I don't want some scumbag who calls himself a minister trying to cover up this situation. I am a man and I'm human,*" Pastor Griffin said.

If I had a dime for every time I was called a scumbag, I'd probably be playing golf with Bill Gates and Warren Buffett. "*You are human and God is forgiving, but the media and your congregation are not.*"

"*Who do you think you are? What gives you the right to profit off of my misfortune? You ought to be ashamed of yourself. You call yourself a minister.*"

"*Look, Pastor Griffin, your pride has been hurt. I get that. You wanted the man to pay, I get that, too, but you're about to lose your entire ministry behind this joker.*"

"*So what are you suggesting that I do?*"

"*This guy is looking for a check. Cut him a check and be done with it.*"

"*That's your big idea. That's what I'm paying you all this money for? Just cut him a check for screwing my wife.*"

"*If you don't make this situation go away he's not only going to screw your wife, he's going to screw you.*"

Pastor Griffin pushed me, and if it weren't for the fact that I had several men standing behind me who kept me from falling, I would've crashed into the wall.

"*Get out of my office!*"

He didn't have to ask me twice to leave, and his wife's lover didn't hesitate to drag his name and his church's name through the dirt. The lover pressed charges. Pastor Griffin got community service, which was a no brainer; the main point was to humiliate the pastor. The lover went on to do a tell-all book that was a scandal throughout the Northeast. Pastor Griffin's situation was proof that everyone pays, even if they don't pay me.

I sat at Joe's Diner across the street from the L.A. Civic Center. The restaurant harkens back to the sixties and I like it because it does not care about its décor as much as its chow. Joe has the best meatloaf in all of Southern California, but in this day and age, that is no longer a selling point when everyone in Southern California is about eating healthy and portion control. I am working on my third cup of coffee when Minister Blackwell arrives.

"God bless, Minister Dungy, it's an honor." Minister Blackwell flashes me a lottery winner's smile and extends his hand.

"How are you?" I say after I shake his hand.

"My, my, my, we had an awesome time tonight at the Faith Fest Convention. Have you ever been?"

"I used to go, but lately I've been too busy," I say as I take a sip of my coffee.

In truth, I stopped going to conferences years ago. To me they are more about egotistical lifts and grandstanding. Furthermore, I stopped being impressed by how a preacher preaches. I know preachers who can cause people to run out of the church and jump into a lake to get baptized. The anointing is strong with the ministers when they are at church, but away from the pulpit they live like the devil. For me the real judge of a person's character is who they are when they are alone with God . . . that, and whether I get the call from a staff member of their church.

"Minister Blackwell, I may be forward in saying this, but can we get down to the reason for this meeting?"

"Well, I first heard about you when you helped Celebration Christian Center."

My mind immediately goes back to Dallas, Texas. Celebration Christian Center has the same situation that Mount Zion has; Pastor Herald did not get up to preach with anything less than a fifth of Jim Beam in his system. While his congregation suspects that he might be under the influence, they will dismiss it because Pastor Herald is a darn good preacher.

When I went to Celebration even I was impressed with how well Pastor Herald was able to preach while inebriated. In the end, Pastor Herald checked into a program and several preachers preach in his stead while Pastor Herald recovers.

"Minister Blackwell, I don't know if my associate told you, but I don't talk about previous jobs."

"Well, did your associate tell you about the money?"

"Yes, but not about the job," I say while trying to be mindful of my voice level.

"Can I get you anything, hon?" A middle-aged blond waitress appears with a pen and note tablet.

"Coffee would be fine," Minister Blackwell says.

"Same here." I hold up my cup as a sign for a refill.

"Well, Minister Dungy, if you could just come up here and observe the situation, you would see what we need your help in. Jubilee Temple is a wonderful church."

"Minister Blackwell, I don't go anywhere without knowing why. I don't care if you offer me a million dollars, if I don't know the problem and everything down to the most minute detail, then I won't take the job. If I feel like you're not being straightforward with me in what's going on, then I won't take the job. Just so we're clear."

My firm policies do not sit well with Minister Black-well; his silence and nervous body gestures convey his displeasure.

"Here you go, hon." The waitress returns and pours both of us a cup of coffee.

I take casual sips of my coffee while I listen to the sounds of tables being bused and mindless chatter from the other patrons in the restaurant.

"Our first gentleman, Tony Robinson, is missing."

"First gentleman?"

"You know, the husband to the pastor who is—"

"Who is a woman, I know. But why is he missing?"

"We don't know. All we know is one night he didn't come home. He hasn't been to church and he hasn't been to work."

"Was there something wrong with their marriage?"

Minister Blackwell's diverted eyes tell it all.

"Tell me or I'll walk."

"There have been rumors that maybe she is having an affair with one of the brothers." Minister Blackwell still doesn't make any eye contact.

"Are they true?"

"No!" Finally Blackwell gives me eye contact.

A woman pastor is a tough sale in this day and age. She represents a progressive movement that believes that Paul's initial rebuke of women teaching is open for interpretation. Still, even in a progressive age where women are at the forefront of social, economic, and political change, a woman pastor is a heavily scrutinized position. To the point where a woman pastor cannot afford any scandal.

"Pastor Robinson is a good woman and an anointed preacher. We don't want anything to happen to her. Will you take the job?"

"No," I say before I took a sip of water.

"That's disappointing. I was led to believe that you would be more forthcoming and sensitive."

"Something tells me that it's not the first time you've been misled; and I'm not sensitive to your situation, which is why I'm good at what I do. I'm able to operate and observe a situation objectively and come up with the best conclusion of how to solve a problem."

Minister Blackwell is beside himself and I understand. I admit that I come off a little mean-spirited, but sometimes it's best to be direct and to the point. Minister Blackwell regains his composure and leans forward to have a more private conversation.

"I heard about the pastor who killed himself in Detroit. The man got caught up in a domestic violence charge. You have anything to do with that?"

"Minister Blackwell, let me be clear that I don't talk about other clients with prospective clients."

"Minister Dungy, if you don't feel that helping this pastor find her husband is a worthy cause, then fine. But consider that we're willing to pay you a lot of money for your trouble. Will you help us?"

Search and rescue is not my forte. Who knew where Pastor Robinson's husband could be, and who knows what details Blackwell is leaving out for this enormous check?

Chapter Seven

I need some direction and God is silent. Maybe God is disappointed in me; maybe I am disappointed in Him. I have come to the one place where I feel like God and I can hash out our differences, Shiloh Temple . The lights are off in the sanctuary and I take a random seat in the middle. I like the fact that I have my pick of any of the 2,000 seats.

The Jubilee job has a big payoff, but the job itself is unchartered territory. A husband who goes rogue can cost a lot of money and time. I am sure that the juice is worth the squeeze. I am also not sure if I should take on another job in light of the fact that I haven't shaken off the loss of Pastor Lewis. I sit in the church with my head bowed and I pray to God for clarity. My sanity holds on by a thread and I need God's help.

While in the midst of my prayer, the lights of the sanctuary come on and footsteps approach my aisle and then stop. I lift my head up and there is Pastor Green with a smirk on his face.

"The more things change the more they stay the same. You still like to pray in the sanctuary with no lights on."

I can say the same for Pastor Green. It has been almost ten years since I left Shiloh and went into the problem-solving business, and Pastor Green still is against wearing suits. Pastor Green loves to wear polo shirts and khaki shorts.

"This is still the best way to hear from God for me," I say.

"I remember when you use to spend hours upon hours laid face down, praying." Pastor Green takes a seat behind me.

I don't look back, but I feel a sense of joy over the good old days when I used to pray for God's guidance. I remember when I used to pray to God to use me to change a life. Lord knows how many lives I've changed over the years, and not for the better.

"That was a long time ago, Pastor Green."

"So what brings you here?" Pastor Green asks.

"I just wanted some alone time with God."

"You don't need to come here for alone time with God, but you already know that. No, I think you're here because you're tired of wandering aimlessly throughout the wilderness."

"You cut right to the chase, Pastor," I say.

"You're the only man I can cut to the chase with. Let's not kid ourselves; you look like you've been dragged through a war zone. You're weary and need rest. I know things went south with you here at Shiloh, but a lot has changed. I have changed and I would love for Shiloh to be your home church again."

I would love for Shiloh to be my home church as well, but the skeptic in me thinks that all Pastor Green wants is an in-house problem solver. I know there is no such thing as a perfect church; I know that better than anyone. I know it, but sometimes I would like to attend a church where I don't know the dirt behind the scenes.

"Do you know if Garland stops by during the day?" I ask.

"He comes by every day for noon prayer."

God bless Garland for being a faithful servant. I admire and envy my friend for his ability to forgive and forget.

"Do you need prayer?" Pastor Green asks.

"Go ahead," I say.

Pastor Green and I pray. I try to block out Pastor Lewis's suicide, the missing first gentleman, and my descent into alcoholism and depression. I try to block all of those roadblocks out and allow the love and grace of God to wash over me, but to no avail.

We conclude our prayer and I do not say another word to Pastor Green. I just get up and walk out of the sanctuary. Just as Pastor Green foretold, Garland is in the hallway, about to enter the sanctuary for noon prayer.

"Nic!' Garland says.

Pastor Green passes me and gives me a pat on the back. "It's good seeing you, Minister Dungy."

"You as well," I say to Pastor Green. I then turn my attention to Garland. "Pick me up by eight forty-five P.M."

Some of my friends used to joke that I had the makings of a serial killer with my obsession for details and order. Whenever I go on a trip I line up every item from the smallest item, being my cufflinks, to the largest item, which is my suit. I begin the process of packing. I already have on my slacks and white undershirt so I put on my watch and collar shirt. I place my wallet in my back pocket and slide on my wool sports coat. I can't afford to leave anything behind; and laying everything out and in order is my way of ensuring that nothing important is left behind. I go to my closet and remove a suitcase that is big enough to hold my clothes, and, at the same time, small enough to fit as a carry-on. I also remove one suit bag. After I pack away my casual clothes and personals, I start to pack my suits.

I decided to take the job. The money is not the primary reason, though the job is quite lucrative. The job has a sense of mystery that reminds me of a Walter Mosley novel, and since this is the closest I will come to being Easy Rawlins, I figure, why not?

I do, however, feel a twinge of guilt that I broke one of my rules. I am convinced that the good Minister Blackwell was not all that forthcoming with information in regard to the details of the job. I make a firm rule not to take a job if I think that my employer has a hidden agenda. There is something that doesn't add up, and in so many ways that is my job: to add things up so that they made sense. As a man who works for God and does not work for a corporate boss, I have to have some rules set in stone. Breaking rules is a luxury I cannot afford.

Part of me wanted to go up North to see some of my old college buddies. I formed lifelong relationships with people I met along the way. I don't have a lot of friends because it's hard for me to trust people. The few friends I have I want to keep, and this job affords me the opportunity to get some sense of normalcy in being able to spend time with my friends.

After I finish packing, I take my suitcase and suit bag into the living room. I set the suitcase down next to the front door and drape the suit bag over the suitcase. I go into the kitchen and I pick up my envelopes of bills. This job can take anywhere from a week to a month depending on what kind of trail the husband left and what exactly happened that made him leave.

I know we live in the twenty-first century and bills can be paid online and I can set things up on auto-pay. However, I can't imagine my vital information being sent across an information superhighway where the future Mark Zuckerberg can steal it and go on a binger. I prefer the old-school method of dropping my bills off at the post office on my way to the airport, and my bills will be paid up for two months.

Now let's see, I got my suitcases and my bills. I realize that I am missing two key elements: my laptop and the file. I go back into the bedroom and grab my laptop bag and the file. I need to review all available information regarding both the church and the pastor. I have to know the church inside and out. There is something that jumps out at me from the file; this is not a large ministry. The church boasts on its Web site of having a large ministry, but from what I gathered there are maybe 600 chairs, which means fewer than 600 people attend the church on a regular basis.

I check the time on my cell phone. I check my watch. The time is 8:37 P.M. I purposely set my watch ten minutes fast because I get physically ill whenever I am late. My ride is supposed to be here by 8:45 P.M.

I am in the middle of my thought when Garland knocks on the door. I place the papers back on the desk and make my way to the living room toward the front door. A six feet three inch husky-framed man darkens my door. Even though I know it is my friend, the image is still frightening.

"You're early," I say as I step away from the door and make my way to the living room. I hear Garland close the door behind him.

"You got everything you need?"

"Just about," I say as I put the printed material in a folder.

"Come on; you're going to miss your flight."

"The last time I was late was in the delivery room," I say as I head toward the front door. Garland helps me with my suitcase and opens the front door for me.

"Thank you, good sir," I say.

Once outside I set my belongings down and wait for Garland to pass, as I lock the door.

"Sometimes I think that you're a vampire because you only travel at night," Garland says.

"If I were a vampire I would've bit you." I chuckle at the thought as I descend the stairs.

Garland is right on my heels, which means that after all of these years of being around me he has finally grasped my need for punctuality. I put my bags in the trunk of Garland's Kia Optima and I make my way toward the passenger seat. I sit and reflect on the questions that still burn in the back of my mind as my body adjusts from the ice-cold air of November to the warmth of Garland's car. Garland gets in the car and does not say a word to me; he just starts the car and makes his way toward the post office down the street from my place.

"Maybe you should take a break after this job," Garland says.

"Can anyone take a break from ministry?" I ask.

Garland allows my question to hang in the air unanswered as he pulls into the post office parking lot located on Avalon.

"Be back in a second." I recall my body moving in a light sprint up the stairs and into the main office, but my thoughts are stuck on rest and vacation. And even though I have enough money saved away where I can travel anywhere in the world and live like a pharaoh for a few weeks, I still feel like I have invisible shackles that prevent me from going anywhere.

I feel more relaxed knowing that tomorrow all of my bills will be sent out to the right collectors, but my walk back is slower. I have half a mind to tell Garland to drop me off at LAX instead and I will take the first flight out to Maui where I can enjoy warm sand, cool water, and breathtaking volcanoes. I don't too much care for waterfalls; volcanoes are a much more rare beauty to behold. I can eat lobster until I get sick and have a drink since nobody will be looking. I would have to find a way to give Minister Blackwell back his money, but that wouldn't be a problem.

Those thoughts carry me to the car. By the time I get back into the car my sense of purpose overrides my sense of adventure. Duty is a word that acts like a double-edged sword: on one end it is used to convey honor and integrity; on the other it is a wound to convey hardship. In the car with Garland I feel the sting of the latter.

"We're all set?" Garland asks as he turns on the car.

"All set," I reply.

Garland maneuvers the car out of the parking lot and we cruise down the street until we enter the 405 freeway.

"So what do you think about the job?" Garland asks.

"Interesting enough. The pay is good and the pastor seems like a genuine person from what I've gathered from the Web site. I just have one question."

"What?"

"Who's paying me?"

Garland thinks it is a stupid question, I'm sure. Of course Garland isn't the type of person to question blessings. I, on the other hand, realize that behind every blessing is a price tag.

"The church." Garland shrugs his shoulders.

"No, it can't be." I shake my head. "The church only has six hundred members on its roster, which means about sixty percent of those members attend service on a weekly basis. Roughly about 275 to 300 people attend the service the most. The average income is fifty thousand dollars. If all three hundred were tithing, which they're not, then that would make their income about $1.5 million. With property costs, maintenance, different ministries, staff salaries, and mainly thirty percent of average church tithing. I come back to my original question. Who is paying me?"

"Maybe you shouldn't be so skeptical," Garland replies.

"One should always have a measure of skepticism. It keeps you from being manipulated. But I'm telling you there's more to this job than what I'm being led to believe."

"So why take the job?"

A fair question, and yet the answer remains elusive to me. "I guess there is something about the job that intrigues me. It's like I can't not take the job no matter how much my mind tells me not to take the job."

And like that, our drive continues in intense conversation followed by awkward silence.

We get off the freeway and I can see the airplanes as they descend to the ground. Airplanes at night remind me of the UFOs I used to see in movies and *Unsolved Mysteries*. As we get close to the departure section, I get a jolt of excitement. I always love a good adventure and I am certain that I am about to go on one today.

"If you need anything, give me a call," Garland says.

"Will do, but you continue to do your thing," I say.

The car stops in front of JetBlue and Garland and I exchange hugs while I grab my bag.

"Have a safe trip," Garland says as he goes back to the car.

"See you when I get back," I say as I take out a cigarette and smoke.

It will be two hours before I can have another cigarette. My flight leaves in forty-five minutes and it is an hour-and-ten-minute flight. As I stand outside inhaling the cool night air and exhaling the menthol from cigarettes, I wonder if I will come back or if this will be the last time I see Garland and my place in Carson?

Chapter Eight

I enter the plane and slide through the narrow space between the rows. I take my seat near the front of the plane because I have to be one of the first people off the plane when it lands. I put my suitcase in the overhead compartment and I take my seat next to the aisle. I have no desire for a window seat. There isn't a beautiful sight for me to behold at ten o'clock at night. My job starts from the moment I accept the assignment until the completion of that assignment.

From the time the FASTEN SEATBELT sign goes off until the time the light will come back on, I am in research mode. I read through as much information as I could get from the Web site, and a few published articles. My file is razor thin and in-between the humble beginnings of a church and the disappearance of the first gentleman is a Grand Canyon of information missing. Like, where is the bulk of the church's revenue stream coming from? Why is Pastor Robinson's ministry so geared to help distraught women? I will need to fill in the blanks as I go along.

The first gentleman thought his wife had an affair with a musician, and I will need to pull out information on the musician as well. I wonder what happened that would make a man disappear. Minister Blackwell made mention of rumors of the affair. Most men I know would've turned the church out in the process, but to vanish is strange and I couldn't wrap my brain around what happened. This job will take more than a week unless I seek help. I have to use discretion, but a missing person and an affair is a concoction that I alone can't handle.

The plane lands an hour and fifteen minutes later after a brief delay caused by an incompetent flight attendant inexperienced at opening the doors. I make my way through a quiet Sacramento airport. Most of the shops and restaurants are closed except for the bar. I could use a drink, but that will need to wait.

Since I have only one suitcase and one suit bag that is big enough to fit in the overhead compartment, I don't worry about baggage claim. I make my way to the rental car agency where I already have a car reserved. I am no stranger to the Sacramento area so I elected to rent a car as opposed to having my point man drive me around an unfamiliar city. Unlike other jobs, I have an advantage with the fact that this job takes place in Sacramento. I have my contacts and I can cover a lot of ground in a short amount of time. I step outside to a somewhat warm night and I wait for the shuttle to arrive so that it can transport me to the rental car place.

It is about ten minutes before the shuttle arrives. I step on the bus and begin my journey to the rental car agency. The ride is no more than seven minutes, but it feels like the shuttle takes forever to navigate through the traffic and turn down a narrow road. I am ready to get my car and go. In fact, I don't even place my suitcase on the shelf; I sit with my suitcase on my lap and my briefcase on top.

When we arrive at the rental car site, I get off the first shuttle and I do a slight jog to Dollar Rent A Car. A young Latina does data entry on her computer until she sees me approach.

"Good evening, sir. Welcome to Dollar Rent A Car."

"I have a reservation," I say as I hand the girl a printed-out version of my confirmation.

"Thank you," she says while she inputs my information. "And do you have your—"

I hand her my ID and other information before she even finishes.

"Thank you." The rep takes the information and makes eye contact with me while she inputs my information. "Here you go." She hands me my ID and a pamphlet with the keys. "The car is out back."

"Thank you." I grab my things and head outside. Once outside I find a cherry red Camry. The car is too flashy, but I love the Camry for the purpose of completing my assignments. The car has room and is reliable. Space and consistency in my field is equivalent to speed and accuracy in any sport.

The congested rental car parking lot is all that resembles Los Angeles. As I drive out of the parking lot and onto the freeway, I see a city that is unchanged through the persistence of time. There are tall buildings, gas stations, fast food restaurants, and Walmart, but for the most part Sacramento remains a massive farmland. Life seems to operate at a slower pace in Sacramento as opposed to its sibling. The 80 freeway is not well lit so I rely heavily on my lights, as opposed to the skyscrapers and the Staples Center that light up Los Angeles. I see my exit, Fernrock, and I take the snakelike exit to the surface streets and arrive at the executive-stay hotel.

I know I have spent too much time on the road when I can pull into a parking lot of a familiar hotel and feel like I am home. I guess that means that my apartment in Carson is nothing more than a permanent hotel room. I pull into an empty parking space and turn off the car. I rest my head back on the seat and take in deep breaths and I exhale. This will be one of a few moments when I am able to rest and relax before I enter the chaotic world of problem solving.

I open a crack in the window to let the smoke out. I don't know if I am addicted to smoking or if I just find comfort in it. Life carries with it many challenges and twists and turns. Stress can produce cancer cells just like smoking, so it is a catch-22 all around. I can't worry about the multiplicity of ways that I can die; that is unproductive.

After I finish my cigarette, I flick the butt into the night as I exit the car. I follow the neon lights of the executive stay and enter an empty lobby.

"Welcome to Executive Suites," the cheerful girl at the help desk says.

"Reservations under Nicodemus Dungy." I hand her all of my documentation.

It takes her only a minute to process my reservation. Preparation is the key for me and I can't expect to be successful if I can't even book a decent hotel.

"Here you go." She hands me both my ID and my room key. "The elevator is to the left."

"Thank you and good night." I make my way to the elevator and on to the second floor where I find my room on the other end of the hall.

After a couple of failed attempts, the key finally grants me access. I open the room door and turn on the lights. The room has a living room with a TV, wet bar, and a desk. The bedroom is in the next room. This room is designed for both business and pleasure. I systematically start to unpack and hang all my clothes up in the closet and lay out all of my valuables in order from wallet to watch along the dresser in my bedroom.

I take a peek at the wet bar and figure that since the church will pick up the tab on my hotel room, I might as well have a glass of Jack Daniel's before I go to bed. Sometimes I'll read the Word and go to bed. Other times I read the Word with single malt and go to bed. I know that God doesn't approve of my drinking, but I have seen some things that would shake anyone's faith. My faith hasn't been destroyed, but it has been damaged to the point where I feel like I need more than prayer to get by.

I read a passage from the Book of Nehemiah. This book has a lot to do with rebuilding. I know that there are areas of my life that have been broken. I grew up in a broken home where my mother left my father. I grew up in a broken neighborhood where decadence reigned supreme and I work in a ministry that is broken by idol worship of its leaders. The inside of my stomach has a burning sensation both from the Jack and the burning sensation that came from the Word. That is the last recollection I have before I go to bed.

At two in the morning I am awakened from a light sleep by an urgent knock. I fumble my way, half asleep, from the bed to the urgent knock. I open the door to find Minister Blackwell on the other side.

"What happened?" I asked.

"She wants to see you."

It takes me a moment to figure out who she is until I realize that "she" is Pastor Robinson. I open the door wide enough to let Minister Blackwell inside the hotel room. I turn on the lights as I close the door.

"I need you to come with me," Minister Blackwell says.

"What happened to tomorrow at eleven A.M.?" I am supposed to meet with Pastor Robinson tomorrow at the church when the sun is out.

"She doesn't want to wait."

"Where are we going?"

Minister Blackwell hesitates to answer. Minister Blackwell is a pushover; anyone can see that, so I decide to be devious. I walk toward Minister Blackwell and he backs up until the heel of his foot touches the wall.

"Okay, I'm not going anywhere until you tell me."

"Minister Dungy, may I remind you that we're paying you a lot of money and—"

"And may I remind you that my contract requires full disclosure."

Minister Blackwell grumbles and mumbles under his breath, "The Sunset Inn."

Unless there is an all-night revival that I have never heard of, the Sunset Inn does not sound like a religious event; it sounds like a sleazy motel. *Okay, now I am game to go and check this whole situation out.*

"Give me a minute," I say before I close the door and throw on my slacks and sport coat. Moments later, I walk out the door and follow Minister Blackwell down the hallway.

Nothing is said while we walk to the elevator. In fact we are silent in the elevator as well. I observe Minister Blackwell, who doesn't appear to be nervous nor on the edge. He does appear to be a little stiff-necked, but I believe that is his natural disposition.

We walk outside into the night cool air. It's not as cold as it is in Detroit, but it is cold nonetheless. Minister Blackwell turns off the alarm of his black Cadillac with his keys. Even his car lacks personality. I get into the car and the leather interior does not ease my chill factor. The one thing that I will give him credit for is that the good Minister Blackwell is a pretty efficient driver. I almost forget that I am the passenger considering how well Blackwell maneuvers out of the parking lot.

"It takes a lot of dedication to do ministry in the wee hours of the morning," I say and Minister Blackwell does not answer; he just continues to drive. I know what may get his goat. "I'm sure you and your wife have had a lot of fallings-out as a result."

"Lorraine died of ovarian cancer four years ago. No children and nothing else you need to know about me."

Wow, and I thought I was tight. Minister Blackwell is a no-nonsense person. He is different from when we met in Los Angeles. People wear different faces at different times for different people. Minister Blackwell is probably all smiles and jokes and encouraging words on Sunday, but on a Tuesday night in a car with a problem solver, I get to see the real Minister Blackwell.

"We will be there in a few minutes, Minister Dungy," Black says.

We ride along the 80 freeway and it is unnerving to travel along a poorly lit highway, especially when I am unsure of the destination.

The Sunset Inn is a motel located off of the 80 freeway. The motel is perfect for a slasher film but what I discover when I arrive is not a psycho serial killer running loose but women in short skirts and revealing clothes escorting desperate men into one of their rooms. I can only imagine why I or anyone a part of Jubilee ministry is here at 2:30 A.M. Minister Blackwell seems comfortable in this element.

"This way, Minister." The minister marches onto the grounds without the slightest hesitation. I follow him with my eyes wide open.

It is a shame to see women so dejected that the only way they can get by is by using their body as a scheme. I feel equally appalled by the clientele. What can cause a man with a good job and family to seek comfort with a desperate woman?

"Hey, handsome, you want to party?" a woman says to me. The woman's hair is a carrot orange and her skin-tight black skirt is way too short in the front. I ignore the woman's advances and follow Minister Blackwell to the room door.

Minister Blackwell knocks on the door and a young woman opens the door. She puts one finger over her mouth for us to be silent. She then uses the other hand to bring us in.

"Thank you, Father." A heavyset woman says as she holds the hands of one of the prostitutes in a hot pink spandex dress with splits along the side.

The heavyset woman has tears flowing down her face and words of fire flow from her tongue. I felt the omni-presence of God fill the room, and only an eternal being could transform a hotel room used for turning tricks into a holy place of worship.

I bow my head and begin to pray to God. Not only for the sins of the hookers and johns, but for my sins as well. The prayer concludes and the heavyset woman hands the girl about three twenty dollar bills from what I observe.

"Go and get you something to eat, honey. And listen, God loves you. Don't let the devil make you think that this is all that life has for you. You are beautiful and God has a beautiful plan for your life."

The girl in the skin-tight pink spandex skirt takes the money and wipes the tears from her eyes. The young woman who opens the door also escorts the girl out of the door. I am left alone with Minister Blackwell and my client, Pastor Robinson.

I can tell Pastor Robinson has a beautiful personality. She can make any man happy who doesn't mind a woman with a little extra weight.

"One night a month I come here. I rent a room and my people pretend to be clients and lure the girls in. Anyone who doesn't want to stay can leave, but those who want to hear the good news, well, I pay them for their time and I pray for them." Pastor Robinson takes a seat on the bed and crosses her legs. "There are at least twenty women who go to the church that was walking the track when I met them."

I give Pastor Robinson a lot of credit. She is a maverick by most religious circles. I like her because she had tremendous confidence and belief in her calling.

"So you're the one who they call Mr. Clean?" Pastor Robinson asks me.

"People can call me whatever they want. I go by Nic or Minister Dungy if I'm feeling ecclesiastical."

Pastor Robinson lets out a chuckle. Her laugh resembles a squeal and she covers her mouth out of embarrassment. It takes Pastor Robinson a moment to gather herself. "I just want you to know that when Minister Blackwell presented me with this idea I was opposed to it."

Now I feel like I am in a motel and it is time for me to get down to business. "Most pastors do and I understand if you want to resolve this issue on your own."

That is what I love about this job. I agreed to help the church and as a result the church had to put up half the money. If Pastor Robinson decides that she no longer wants my services, well, then I just got $75,000 richer without breaking a sweat. But Pastor Robinson will not back out; she just wants to air her reservations in order to save face.

"Well, it would be a waste to bring you out here for nothing, so how does this work?" Pastor Robinson says.

I sink my hands into my pockets and walk over to Pastor Robinson. I make sure that my shoulders are up and that I do not give the slightest hint of insecurity. "I need full disclosure. I need to know everything, before I can do anything."

Pastor Robinson uncrosses her legs and folds her hands. "What do you want to know?"

"The last night you saw your husband."

"Two weeks ago we had an argument. He thought that I had been neglecting him and I guess the rumors started to get to him. He wanted me to take some time away from ministry to work on our marriage."

"I guess you said no; otherwise, I wouldn't be here."

Pastor Robinson did not respond. I have seen too many occasions where ambition has robbed marriages and blinded leaders. Pastor Robinson is no exception.

"Were the rumors true?"

"No," Pastor Robinson says.

"Don't lie to me. Don't ever lie to me. If the rumors are true then let me know and I will still help, but don't lie to me or I walk." I walk up toward Pastor Robinson so that she can know that I'm not playing. "Now I'm going to ask one more time, are the rumors true?"

"No! They're not. They are evil lies made up by my detractors," Robinson says with a look of discontent.

"So why would your husband give into the rumors? It has to be more than your husband feeling neglected. Most pastors neglect their spouses; it's in the bylaws."

"Jeremy is not only a promising basketball player, but he is a skilled musician. I have bragged about him to the point where it started to arouse suspicion and no man can handle their wife talking about another man more than them. So what should we do?" Pastor Robinson asks.

"I suggest that Pastor continues to do as she's been doing. She continues to preach the Gospel while you locate her husband and talk some sense into him," Minister Blackwell says.

"Really? That's funny. I was about to suggest the opposite. In fact we're going to do the exact opposite," I reply.

"I don't want to draw attention to his absence," Minister says.

"There is already attention being paid to her husband's absence. I'm not just a Mr. Fix-it; I am a minister and when I step into a situation I look to resolve it. I neither take nor do I have repeat customers. There's your way of doing things and then there is my way of doing things, which is the right way."

So after I put Minister Blackwell back in his place, I then turn my sights to Pastor Robinson, who is eager to hear my suggestions. "Once I find your husband I can guarantee you that there is nothing I could say that will repair things. You'll have to do that on your own. So I want you to still preach the special events that you made commitments for, but I want you to turn over your weekday and weekend services to some of your other ministers."

I can tell that Pastor Robinson really takes heed to my words. I pray that I will be successful in my endeavor. I hate to lose more than anything, especially in the arena of ministry.

"So what happens now?" Pastor Robinson asks.

"First Minister Blackwell is going to drive me back to my hotel so I can get some sleep. Then I am going to return in the morning to the church and start to do my work. I will need for you to pull any information you have on your husband. Check stubs, identification, articles, you name it."

"Okay," Pastor Robinson says.

"Great! See you tomorrow." I head toward the door knowing that this meeting provided new information that has my head spinning with the possibilities of what could've happened to the first gentleman.

"Wait!" Pastor Robinson says before I reached the door.

My back is still turned. I look back to see Pastor Robinson still on the bed.

"What are we supposed to say when the congregation starts to see you around a lot?"

"The truth. That I'm a visiting minister who's here to serve Jubilee Temple."

And that is not a lie. I am a minister who is here to serve both the church and my own interests.

Chapter Nine

I wake up the next morning around 7:30 A.M. I forgot to close the curtains in my hotel room, so the sun makes its presence known in my room and I cannot afford to sleep in. I have to do my job so I get up and stretch. My shirt, tie, and sports coat are draped over the chair. Last night I slept in my slacks and my white undershirt. Since I am half dressed I grab my watch, wallet, and room key off the table, slip on my shoes, and head out door. I'll brush my teeth and wash my face later. I hate the aftertaste of eating right after I have brushed my teeth.

I take the stairs instead of the elevator and that will be my exercise for today. The weather is sunny and brisk and since we are in the middle of November, I know that the good weather won't last. By noon the weather will be overcast and I can tell by the way the clouds are gathering in the sky that there might even be rain.

I walk across the street to Lane's Diner. I have not eaten since yesterday afternoon so I need some type of food in my system. It's real easy for me to forget to do simple things like eat, shave, or sleep when I'm on a job.

"Hello, welcome to Lane's. Is this a party of one?" The hostess has already grabbed a menu.

"Actually, I know what I want and I need it to go."

"Okay," the girl says, somewhat surprised.

It is not often, I assume, she encounters a man who knows what he wants.

"Go ahead to the counter and they'll place your order there."

I walk over to the counter, but I don't take a seat. I get the attention of the waitress and she comes over right away.

"What can I get for you, sir?"

"Two eggs over easy, hash, bacon, and sourdough toast." I go into my wallet and place a twenty on the counter.

"Okay, let me get two eggs over easy, hash, bacon, and sourdough toast coming up and you can pay up front with cashier."

"That's for you." I point to the twenty dollar bill.

"Thank you, sir. A girl could use it."

I consider myself a part of the same industry as the waitress. We both are in the service industry, but while she serves patrons, I serve the church. I pay the bill on the way out and I walk across the street to the gas station on the corner. I need a pack of cigarettes. I crave a cigarette and I am low on my pack I bought yesterday.

"Let me get a pack of Newports," I tell the attendant.

The gas attendant grabs a pack of Newports and sets them on the counter. I slide a twenty dollar bill under the window and the attendant slides back my change and my cigarettes.

I walk back over to Lane's restaurant and I pick up my breakfast. I also order a cup of coffee to go. With breakfast, coffee, and a pack of smokes in hand, I'm ready to start my day. So I walk back to my hotel room. Back at my hotel room, minutes from the meeting at last night's roadside motel play on repeat in my mind.

I can see both the appeal and controversy that surrounds Pastor Robinson. She has an edge to her ministry that can spark admiration from her followers and scorn from her critics. I can tell that her disposition is that she doesn't care either way. Pastor Robinson is a woman of purpose and not even her husband, Tony Robinson, can derail her purpose.

I want to go by the church and get a feel for how the church works. Sundays are not a good measuring stick for a ministry. The staff is usually on their best behavior when visitors are around. It is during the week when I can get a good feel for how a ministry operates. If the right people are in place then a ministry can weather any storm, but the wrong people serving in ministry is a cancer to a church.

Too many relatives, too many well-meaning but incompetent people are millstones around the necks of a ministry. I have seen it happen too often and the worst part is that these internal issues will leave the church defenseless against the enemy.

I am not here to restructure a ministry, but I have no problems leaving notes for how a ministry can clean house when I am gone. I finish my breakfast and get dressed. My next stop is Jubilee Temple.

I arrive at Jubilee Temple and am greeted by Anita, the church secretary. Anita is a heavyset girl with thick glasses.

"Good morning and God bless." Anita's words are tailored with warmness. Anita's spirit leaves little doubt as to why she is employed in her current capacity as church secretary.

"Minister Nicodemus Dungy to see Pastor Robinson."

It is awkward to mention my title with my name. I almost forget that I am an ordained minister who graduated from one of the top Bible colleges in the country. My days at seminary seem like a lifetime ago. My vigor is gone and my purpose grows cloudier with age and experience and I grow weary.

"Minister Dungy, thank you for coming." Pastor Robinson comes out in a cherry red pantsuit. Her aura conveys power without a hint of weakness.

"God bless you, Pastor," I say as Pastor Robinson signals for me to follow her to her office. Once I enter Pastor Robinson's office, I become lightheaded by all of the accolades on the wall.

A woman in ministry is always under scrutiny and Pastor Robinson always has to prove herself. Pastor Robinson's office speaks more about her insecurities than it speaks about her anointing. Secure pastors are purpose driven, while insecure pastors are accomplishment driven.

I examine all of the pictures that Pastor Robinson has with influential people and then call my attention to a picture on her desk of her husband. I notice that there are no children in the picture and that this picture was taken when the love was still new and the young girl in the picture was not a prominent pastor.

I pick up the picture and Pastor Robinson shoots me a look as if I have caused a great offense. I have an idea of the kind of love she and her husband once had and how far the two have grown apart.

"So what do you need from me, Minister Dungy?"

"That was something else last night. I've heard of women ministers who minister to women on the track, but I'd never seen it until last night."

"There's nothing that I hate more than a pastor who talks about going out to the lost and preaching the Gospel, but they never do it. Wouldn't you agree, Minister Dungy?"

"Nic."

"Excuse me?"

"Nic, call me Nic. I'm only a minister in title. What you do is ministry." I sit down in the chair positioned in front of Pastor Robinson.

"I would beg to differ."

"So what did Tony think about your ministry?"

"He didn't think anything," Pastor Robinson replies. "He did; otherwise, I wouldn't be here."

"Are snap judgments a part of your method?" Pastor Robinson looks up from her paperwork.

"Pretty much, but that doesn't mean I'm wrong. You have an intense ministry and I can imagine that a loving husband would be concerned about his wife being out all hours of the night evangelizing in some unsafe areas."

"That's the kind of answer I expect from a male minister. But it's okay for you to be out all hours of the night?" Pastor Robinson says.

"I'm not here to engage in a debate with you. You don't like my opinions; well, that's fine, but your husband has left and something tells me that it's not just the rumors of an affair, but your overall involvement in ministry."

"I know you're not married because there's no ring on your finger, but the question is why?" Pastor Robinson asks.

"I'm too smart to get married."

"That's not a biblical perspective on marriage."

"Hey, the Apostle Paul was also smart enough not to get married and he wrote the majority of the New Testament. Paul understood that the preaching of the Gospel requires full dedication."

"Whatever; a husband should be supportive of his wife."

Pastor Robinson resumes her paperwork. The absence of emotion is what bothers me the most about Pastor Robinson. Her husband has disappeared for two weeks and she chooses to hire me as opposed to filing a missing person report.

"Let me ask you something." I put my hands in my pocket.

She responds to me by breaking away from her papers to make eye contact.

"When was the last time you and your husband were intimate?"

"Excuse me?"

"Sex! When was the last time you and your husband had sex?"

"That's none of your business." Pastor Robinson tosses her papers on the table.

"It is when I'm looking for your husband. When a marriage waxes cold, the sex life is one of the first things to break down along with communication."

"You don't beat around the bush now do you?"

"No, I prefer to pull it out by its roots." I shrug my shoulders.

"I couldn't begin to tell you how many months it has been."

"Months?" I shake my head in disbelief. "What happened?"

Pastor Robinson leans back in her chair as if it is too much for her to pinpoint. "It started off as a small space, a missed date night here and there; then it grew into working late until it grew into something that neither one of us wanted to address."

I know Pastor Robinson's speech word for word. I've heard this speech so many times over the years and the saddest thing is that every one of those times I've heard that speech it was sincere. There was no difference in this day and age between a Christian marriage and a secular marriage.

"So what about you, Minister Dungy?"

"What about me?"

"You're a minister of the Gospel and you're single, so how do you resist temptation?"

No one has ever questioned me like Pastor Robinson. Her question was not birthed out of her curiosity about my sex life, no; she asked the question to put me on defense. "I'm a man of God, but I have had moments of weakness where the flesh has won out."

Pastor Robinson is taken aback by my honesty. I'm too old and too tired to play dress-up. My life is not squeaky clean and I'm not ashamed to admit it.

"How do you handle it?"

"I stay busy with work. Speaking of which, I'm going to need the address and phone number to your husband's job."

"He hasn't been to work."

That is the most alarming detail of Tony Robinson's disappearance. I don't know too many men who would miss work on account of their marriage or relationship.

"I'll go anyway and see what's what."

"Okay," the pastor says.

For someone who claims to be innocent of any extra-marital affairs, she sure does not seem innocent. Even more alarming is that the pastor seems unconcerned about her husband's whereabouts.

Chapter Ten

I drive over to Tony Robinson's place of employment. I pull into the parking lot of Orbit Software Company. It seems like the first gentleman has a good job as a software engineer. A good job that isn't worth missing. After I park, I take a moment to review the information that Pastor Robinson has given me. First Gentleman Tony Robinson was born in Richmond, California. His father worked at a sheet metal factory and his mother was a school secretary. Based on the articles from the local newspaper, Tony was a pretty good tailback, but not good enough to go to a Division I school on scholarship. Tony's glory and fame ended in high school. Tony went on to San Jose State and got a degree in engineering. Tony later got a master's degree in the same field, and he lived a normal life until his wife, Alicia Robinson, decided to become a preacher.

I watch as the employees enter and exit through a building that can only be accessed by keycard. There is no way I can get into the building, but I might not need to with the weather in my favor. I was wrong in my earlier assessment; the day has turned out to be clear and there is a light breeze. God only knows how many lovely days like this I waste working.

Outside are a few steel benches with an open umbrella to provide shade. Three women sit in a half circle while they devour their salads, the sun, and conversation.

Tony Robinson is a nice-looking guy and I figure that one of the women will know Tony and provide me with some much-needed information. So I make my way toward the women and make sure that I turn my swagger on and up.

"Hello, ladies," I say.

A few squeals and chuckles and I know that the women lock on to me like a heat-seeking missile.

"I was looking for—"

"Me?" The assumed leader of the pack asks.

I chuckle to myself. I am not a *GQ* model, but I do have an appeal with women with my rugged looks and conservative style of dress. "I'm looking for Tony Robinson."

The women look at each other with curious suspicion. I don't know if my inquiry of the first gentleman sparks controversy or shyness.

"We haven't seen him." The leader of the group looks at the other two women. "We haven't seen him in like a week or two."

"I thought he was on vacation," another girl says.

That is a clever question. The woman wants me to divulge information as it relates to Tony's absence from work, but I am not up for playing that game. These girls don't know any more information than what I have already obtained.

"I don't know. I hadn't seen him in a while and I was looking to catch up with him," the leader said.

"Thank you," I say as I turn away and head toward the car. I don't want to leave a lasting impression; I just want to get the information I need and go. So far the trip to Tony's job is a waste of time.

I am not even to my car when I hear the sound of heavy footsteps. I turn around and a heavyset man who is well over the six-feet, 300-pound mark approaches me. I do not want an altercation, especially with a man who is the size of a bear, but the fact that he approaches me means that I am getting close.

"Why are you asking about Tony?" The guy gets close enough to impose his physical dominance over me.

"I just needed to talk to him."

"You Jesus freaks need to leave him alone." The guy points at my temple.

My animal instinct is to bite his finger off, but I hold my poise. "Actually I owed him a beer and I came by to clear my debt. But since you're here I can settle my debt with you."

Two hours later, and three beers to Mike and four bottles of water to me, and I find myself in the middle of a sports conversation.

"They can't move the Kings to L.A. That would be stupid to have three L.A. teams. Man, these rich folks are a trip. They just make drastic changes without any regard for the little people."

"I agree with you."

I wait for Mike to enjoy another sip of his Heineken. Mike became chatty after the first beer. "Let me ask you something."

Mike signals for me to keep going as he holds the bottle to his lips.

"What would cause Tony to leave his job?"

Mike slams the bottle down with some force. "Look, man, I ain't no snitch"

"I'm neither a cop nor a gangster."

"I've never seen my boy talk to you or talk about you. I've never even seen you before today."

"I'm a concerned individual and I'm trying to help reconcile things between Tony and his wife."

"The broad . . ." Mike catches himself. The alcohol has not tempered his aggression. "She thinks she can help thousands and then disrespect my boy."

"How?"

Mike straightens up his posture and gives me a stern look. "Look, man, I made it a habit to mind my own business and you should do the same."

"I'll keep that in mind, but answer me this: have you seen him recently?"

"About a week ago. He said he needed space. I offered him a place to stay and he said he had a place already."

"Did he say anything about leaving town?"

Mike replies by shaking his head. I give Mike a pat on his back and step away from the bar. I leave a hundred dollar bill on the bar and signal to the Irish bartender that the money is for Mike. Mike gave me some useful information and I have another person to see before I call Pastor Robinson with an update.

From the bar, I drive out to Richmond, California and make my way to Richmond High School.

Richmond High School is home of the Oilers, which is a bitter emblem for an area that is at a socioeconomic disadvantage. The chips are stacked against the students, which leaves them one main area to strike oil: sports. Based on the file, I know that Tony Robinson fought with every inch to climb out of the pit. The only problem is that Tony used the same pipe dream that everyone else uses.

I sit and observe a football practice already in session. A small group of boys and girls hangs out at the bottom of the bleachers. I sit at the top and I try to tune out their mindless, vulgar chatter. Instead I focus my attention on Head Coach Eric Williams. Williams has been the head coach of Richmond High School for nineteen years. His no-nonsense attitude commands respect from his coaching staff and players. Williams stands out on the sideline deck in a white polo, black slacks, and dark shades with his arms folded like Mr. T. I watch as each player tries to execute each play to perfection, and from the look of Coach Williams, he wouldn't accept anything less from his players.

I wait until after practice to approach Coach Williams. Even after Coach Williams sends his team to the showers, Williams still stays back and works with a few of his promising players. I head down the steps of the bleachers and cross the dirt track. I'm sure my $300 shoes do not like getting dirt on them, but I have a job to do. Once I cross the track, I am in Coach Williams's radar.

"Can I help you?' Coach Williams says.

"Yes. My name is Minister Nicodemus Dungy and I had a few questions to ask you about Tony Robinson."

Williams maintains his poker face despite the fact that I have just mentioned one of his prized players. Williams starts to walk and I start to follow.

"What do you want to know about Tony?"

"I just wanted to know if you've seen him lately."

My question causes Coach Williams to stop dead in his tracks. "I may have been born at night, but it wasn't last night. If you can't find Tony then that means he doesn't want to be found."

"He may not want to be found, but he needs to. His wife is worried sick."

Coach Williams chuckles to himself as he reaches into his pocket and pulls out a bag of sunflower seeds and pours some in his mouth. I can tell that Coach Williams wants to tell me something, but he needs a reason to trust me.

"Listen, I know you're loyal to him, but I needed to know if you have either seen or heard from him recently. That's it, nothing more."

Williams spits out some of the seeds on the grass. "He came by here about a week ago. He looked like he was upset about something."

"Did he tell you what about?" I ask.

"I didn't ask and he didn't say. He just sat and watched the practice and gave a few pointers to the young bucks. That was it."

And that is all I need. Between Michael and Eric, I am able to establish a timeline that the last anyone has seen or heard from Tony was a week ago.

"Thank you, Coach, and good luck with the season." I shake hands with Coach Williams and start to walk away.

"He couldn't handle pressure," Coach Williams says.

"Excuse me?'

"Tony. He couldn't handle pressure. That's why he didn't make it. Put him in a game with nothing to lose and Tony was phenomenal, but in the close games and the games that counted for something, he'd fold like a bad hand. You know what I mean?"

"I believe I do." I step away from Coach Williams to make a phone call.

"Hello," Pastor says on the other end.

"It's Nic. I found out that your husband is still in town."

There is a brief silence that could be interpreted to mean many things.

"Okay, so what happens now?" she finally asks.

"Now I go and see a friend," I reply.

"Can he find him?"

"He can find for you a burning bush."

"He could find a burning bush?" Pastor Robinson chuckles, but I don't because I know that the guy I am going to see is that good.

Chapter Eleven

Spider is a six foot white boy decorated in tattoos from his neck down to his arms. He wears a black Oakland A's baseball cap and a black sweatshirt. Some of his tattoos can't be covered with a hood sweatshirt, and creep out the sides of his neck and hands. Arguably, Spider is the best bounty hunter on the West Coast.

Spider grew up in Lexington, Kentucky, where hunting is as much of a necessity as chores and church. I met Spider fifteen years ago in college, where he studied criminal justice. At first I thought he was a classic tale of a white boy who wanted to be black, but Spider has an edge and realness to him. Spider dropped out of college after his sophomore year and started experimenting with drugs. I found Spider five years ago at the MacArthur BART station begging for change. After an extensive conversation, he got saved.

That seems like a lifetime ago. Spider is unable to become a lawyer because he has a criminal record. He then decided to go into law enforcement, and became a bounty hunter. Today, Spider serves cookies to underprivileged kids. He volunteers with an inner-city program as a way to tap into the softer side of an otherwise tough exterior.

I know working to catch criminals can take its toll on an individual, so volunteering at community centers reminds Spider that he is helping to create a better environment for these children.

"Argh!" a little kid yells as he runs toward Spider.

Spider picks the boy up by one hand and holds him to the ceiling. "I got you now."

"I'm stronger than you," the little kid says as he tried to squirm out of Spider's massive grip.

Moments later, Spider puts the little kid down and is relieved of his duties by this Hispanic lady and proceeds to take out the trash. I figure this is a good time to approach Spider. I follow him outside of the building, where there is a beat-up Dumpster with chipped paint that is waiting to be filled. Spider's back is turned.

"You think in a room filled with kids I can't spot an unshaved man in a suit?"

I follow his smart remark with a playful combination to the ribs. In a real fight, where I gave up four inches in height and fifty pounds in weight, I would've been beaten to a point beyond recognition. Spider welcomes the playful exchange with a combination of his own before giving me a hug.

"What's up, brotha?" Spider says. He breaks away and examines me. "You look like crap, as usual."

"What can I say? It suits me."

"So what are you doing here?" Spider tosses the garbage bag into the Dumpster.

"Work. I'm helping a church out."

Spider fixes his lips. Though he does not know what I do officially, Spider knows that I am not a straight-laced preacher.

"So why are you out here in San Leandro? You missed me?"

"Of course not." I shrug my shoulders. "I got a job for you."

"A job? What kind of job?" Spider asks.

"One that suits your particular skill set."

"What, a member of the church stole the offering?" Spider lets out a laugh and I let out a smirk.

"Is he or she running from the law?" Spider asks.

"Worse, his wife."

Spider lets out a sadistic laugh. "That may be harder to find."

"I figured that." I reach into my jacket and remove an envelope and toss it to Spider. "That's ten grand. Half now, half when the job is complete."

Spider opens the envelope and examines the stack of one-hundred-dollar bills. Missing persons is not my thing. I moonlight as a minister, so if I pay Spider twenty grand from a hundred fifty grand to find Tony Robinson, it is worth it.

"That's a lot of scratch to find a husband."

"What can I say? She really wants to reconcile things. Listen, I just need you to knock on a couple of doors. Check the airports, bus depots, to see if he might've left town. We'll get together later and compare notes."

"Okay, I got you. When was the last time she saw him?" Spider puts the envelope in his front pocket.

"Two weeks ago."

Spider lets out a whistle. He and I both know the complexity that comes with a search for a man who has gone missing for more than two weeks. "He could be anywhere."

"I spoke with his coworker and his coach. He's still here in town, I think. At least, he was a week ago."

"If he's here, I'll find him. I'll need information."

I reach into my jacket and pull out another envelope that has more information in it. I spent last night compiling information from Tony Robinson's driver's license and bank statements. Name it and I have it in the file. Pastor Robinson was instrumental in my acquisition of the information; she did not spare any information.

"Okay. I'll get started. But if he's skipped town, then you got to make travel arrangements for me to get him."

"I can manage that." I shrug my shoulders again.
*Now that I have Spider-man on the trail, the rest of
this job will be a piece of cake.*

I arrive back at the church and enter a midsized sanctuary. The pulpit has a one-step platform with a diamond-
shaped middle where the pulpit is located. There are pews
with purple padding that matches the drapes. Purple is a
color of divinity, royalty, and the Los Angeles Lakers, but
it is not a color that summons men. I wish that men didn't
pay attention to such trivial things as the décor of a church,
but they do. We're taught to walk by faith and not by sight,
but that biblical principle is easier said than done.

I walk into a meeting already in progress. Pastor
Robinson, Minister Blackwell, and a man who I have not
previously met are in the front pew. The man gets up and
walks over to me.

"Hi, I'm Minister Mackie." He shakes my hand. "I feel
like I'm meeting Davy Crockett."

"I'm not sure if I should take it as a compliment." I'm
not used to people being happy to see me. I am usually
treated like a necessary family event. People are nervous
and on edge when I'm here and happy when I am gone.

"Well, it's because you're about to make the devil mad."
Minister Mackie flashes me a Kool-Aid smile.

The rest of the people in the room do not share Minister Mackie's enthusiasm. I feel like I make the devil laugh
more than anything with my futile attempts. It is only
on those rare occasions when I make a connection with
my clients that it feels like I am doing real damage in the
kingdom.

"So what's up?"

"We have a problem," Minister Blackwell says.

"Well, we don't have time to fool around so let's hear
it."

"The associate pastor is not ready," Pastor Robinson says sternly.

This is the part that I hate the most about my job: pastors and their authority. A pastor who is full of pride is very toxic in this kind of situation, where they have to take direction from someone else. I put my hands in my pockets and walked over to Pastor Robinson. "And why is the associate pastor not prepared to assume a role that he was supposed to be prepared for?"

"Because I made him the associate pastor without any intentions of him taking over in my absence. In the beginning it was hard to get someone to be committed to a woman pastor. Mitchell was committed and I made him Pastor. It was an emotional decision and not a spiritual one and I realize that now."

Pastor Robinson made a common problem that so many pastors make. They make decisions based on emotions and rationale. Rarely do they take into account what God's Word says about wisdom and using wisdom and spiritual conviction during the process of picking leaders.

"So what's wrong with him?" I ask.

"He doesn't have good communication skills."

I laugh to myself and begin to pace the floor. A pastor with poor communication skills is the same as a baseball player with no hand-to-eye coordination. It's a small wonder how this ministry grew to its current size given that so many poor decisions were made in the flesh and not the spirit. The three ministers shake their heads and look at each other.

"Is Bible Study tonight?" I ask.

"At seven P.M.," Minister Blackwell says.

"I'll sit in and observe how things run and we'll go from there," I reply.

"Okay," Pastor Robinson says.

I can tell that Pastor Robinson is reluctant to give up her pulpit, but I can't consider her feelings while trying to resolve her issue.

"May I have a moment with Pastor Robinson?" I say to Minister Blackwell and Minister Mackie.

Minister Blackwell and Minister Mackie look at Pastor Robinson, who then gives them a head nod and the two men leave without any resistance. I wait until the men have left the sanctuary before I go and have a seat along the front pew. I tap an empty space on the pew for Pastor Robinson to have a seat next to me, and she does after a moment of hesitation.

"I have to be honest with you; your ministry is not in the best of shape," I say.

"You should've seen the look on folks' faces when I told them God called me to the ministry. I still remember what I had on: a black T-shirt with hot pink in the design. I also had the hot pink shorts to match and, boy, was they short."

I chuckle because even in the most progressive church, Pastor Robinson's outfit would've been unacceptable.

"But God called me and I answered the call, but no one wanted to support me in ministry except for Pastor McMurray, Minister Blackwell, and Minister Mackie. They stuck with me through thick and thin and I rewarded them for that."

"I can imagine how hard it must've been for you, but when it's God's will, you have to trust that even when it looks grim."

Pastor Robinson has tears and she reaches into her suit jacket and removes some tissue. Pastor Robinson wipes her eyes and I can tell that her tears are not over who she named Associate Pastor.

"Sometimes I hate being good at my job," I say, but I don't wait for a response. "I can tell when someone's lying and I can tell when someone is hiding something."

"Minister Dungy, I don't have time for this. If you have something to say then say it."

"You need to make time, but all I've observed in the brief time that I have been here is that you're less concerned about finding your husband than you are about who teaches tonight's Bible Study."

Pastor Robinson avoids eye contact with me. She just sits there with her head down. "Tony was against me going into the ministry. Sometimes my husband can throw a fit like a little kid. It took awhile for him to let me go to seminary. I think he figured that I would quit just as soon as it got hard like I did with everything else." Pastor Robinson shakes her head and chuckles to herself. "I showed him, and even now, he still has his reservations; but I thought we were past this."

There is something in her tone and her words that convey to me a cryptic message. Pastor Robinson is not beside herself over her husband's disappearance. "This isn't the first time he has left has he?"

Pastor Robinson shakes her head. "Nope. This is the longest, but Tony has a habit of disappearing for a week. Then he shows up and doesn't want to talk about where he's been. I put up with it because he's my husband and I love him."

Pastor Robinson wipes her eyes. "I forgive him and I try to refocus my attention on the ministry. Tony leaving is his way of getting back at me for not doing things his way, but this latest disappearing act is his longest."

"So you're thinking he'll come back?"

"Of course, because he's in love," Pastor Robinson replies.

"So then why hire me?" I shrug my shoulders.

"Because I'm not some naïve twenty-three-year-old who ain't got anything better to do than run behind some man. I have a ministry to run and I was told that you're good at handling these matters discreetly."

"I can and I will, but I need for you to be ready to know what to say to your husband when I do find him."

"So your friend is looking for him?" Pastor Robinson asks.

"He's on the case and you should be ready to reconcile with your husband."

"I am." Pastor Robinson rolls her eyes.

"I hope for your sake you're right."

"God bless you and welcome to Jubilee." A beautiful greeter leads me to an usher who leads me to the sanctuary. I enter the sanctuary and see the praise team engaged in praise and worship while one-third of the congregation sit and clap their hands. I take a seat at the back pew. To me the best seat in the house is the back of the church. I find out a lot about a church and its effectiveness from the back row. I can tell if someone pays attention to the service or if they just text. I can even read the faces of the people sitting in the pulpit and tell if they are into the service, as well. The back row gives me the most objective view of the church.

Pastor Robinson sits in her chair with a Bible on her lap. She looks prepared to preach, and only time will tell if Robinson will play ball. At the musician station I notice the drummer, Jeremy, stare at Pastor Robinson like a work of art. Jeremy is about as subtle as a marching band.

"You notice that this is like the third week since First Gentleman has been here?" an elderly sister of the church says to another woman.

"I hear that he left the pastor for another woman. Most men can't handle an anointed woman."

I start to chuckle, loud enough to get the two women's attention and to get the women to shut up. The women have the nerve to look offended and I have the nerve to look at them like they are crazy.

"Praise the Lord. To God be the glory!" Minister Blackwell says. "Give an honor to God and our praise team is anointed."

I let out a smirk. So many Christians speak in Christianese and their halfhearted replies do not move me.

"Well, it's time to eat. Let's give an honor to our associate pastor, Pastor McMurray." Minister Blackwell starts clapping and the sanctuary turns hollow. Whenever a church has a pulpit hog, the members become skeptical of hearing anyone else.

Pastor McMurray approaches the pulpit. He looks nervous, which is somewhat understandable. Based on Pastor Robinson's assessment of McMurray's communication skills, he is not used to being in front of a group of people, no matter how small of a group.

"Lord, let the words of my mouth and the meditation of my heart be acceptable in thy sight."

Amen.

The associate pastor concludes the prayer and I can see pages of the Bible turn. I even hear devices being powered on and Bibles pulled up. The scripture will be taken from Proverbs 4. Proverbs 4 is a smart choice for a passage of scripture that focuses on wisdom.

It is not long before the pastor starts sweating profusely. I am at the back of the sanctuary and I can see it. It kind of reminds me of the time my parents took me to SeaWorld and how the front row was reserved for people who really wanted to get wet by Shamu.

"And, see . . . see . . . see the Bible . . ." Nothing in Pastor McMurray's speech indicates that he has a speech impediment, but, boy, when he starts to stutter, the members of the congregation start to hold up one finger and make an abrupt exit.

Jeremy gets up and heads out of the sanctuary. I think that this will be a good time to fact check Pastor Robinson's story. Pastor Robinson claims that there is nothing going on between her and Jeremy. I need to see for myself. I get up and follow Jeremy out of the sanctuary and outside of the church.

I keep a safe distance as I follow Jeremy around the corner. The church is located in a former industrial building and thus is surrounded by industrial buildings.

I follow Jeremy around a carpentry building and discover that Jeremy is about to light something that isn't a cigarette. Jeremy is startled when he sees me out of his periphery.

"Oh shoot! My bad, man."

"Oh, no need to apologize. I snuck up on you," I say as I take another step.

"I've been struggling with this for a while." Jeremy holds up the joint. "I keep praying for God to take the taste out of my mouth."

Like I said, most Christians have perfected Christianese and not the Christian way of living. Jeremy could quit smoking weed anytime he gets ready. Jeremy struggles because he wants to, just like I give in to a lot of my vices.

"You're a minster who's visiting aren't you? Pastor Robinson told me."

"Are you and Pastor Robinson close?" I asked.

"She's real supportive of me," Jeremy says and I can see the admiration on his face.

What I also see is a small smile creep from his mouth. Jeremy zones out as if he is reliving a good dream or fantasy.

"What about Mr. Robinson?" I ask.

"What?" Jeremy snaps out of his fantasy.

"The first gentleman, Tony Robinson. Is he also supportive of you?"

Jeremy sits there and shakes his head. "No, not really. He doesn't say anything to me. And I don't say anything to him, but he's cool though."

Jeremy's words are weighed by bitterness. Jeremy never makes eye contact, which means that he either has poor manners or that he is hiding something.

"Do you have a girlfriend?" I ask.

Jeremy laughs at my absurd question. "Naw, man, I don't. I'm focused on my school, playing ball, and my relationship with God."

"But you are in love with someone aren't you?" I ask, and my question causes Jeremy to zone out again.

"I don't know! I don't know what I feel. It's just crazy to feel something and not know what it is."

I extend my hand and, after a moment, Jeremy hands me the joint. I put it out under my foot. "I hear you're a terrific basketball player with a bright future."

"Yeah. I want to go to Duke," Jeremy says.

"A bit of advice: leave things that can hinder your career alone. You see in the news all the time athletes with extraordinary abilities and huge character flaws. Your talent will only take you so far; your character will take you the rest of the way. If God has given you a vision then God will complete it, so long as you stay on the right path."

Jeremy is a smart kid. He knows exactly what I am talking about and he gives me a head nod. I still am not sure if there is an affair that exists between Jeremy and Pastor Robinson, but at least now I know why Tony Robinson might be jealous of this young man. Jeremy represents who Tony used to be.

Chapter Twelve

Most nights I am restless. I don't toss and turn in the bed; I just lie there on my back and stare at the ceiling in the dark. My mind can't seem to settle down. I am too locked into the case and all of the different scenarios that play out in my head to sleep. Luckily, I can perform my job with very little sleep.

When I am asleep that is when the night terrors come. I have dreams of a minister; at least, I assume he is a minister, judging by the traditional clergy robes he wears. He has no eyes, no way I can look at his eyes or judge him. I can't explain why I have no room to move. It is not like the minister is deformed, but still I can't escape. I punch at the figure and my hands feel like wet paper bags punching against marble. I know this is a dream, but the terror feels real and my heart tries to escape from my chest.

I wake up and sweat has drenched my shirt and my forehead. I roll out of bed and I fall to my knees. "Lord, I need you. I need your peace, which surpasses all understanding. I need your peace, give me peace! Lord!"

I try to pray, but images implode within my brain. I get up and I go over to the wet bar and I grab a few miniatures of that brown liquor. I take the miniature bottles by the throat and twist the cap. I bypass a cup and knock back the first bottle and then the second one.

I have little tolerance for weakness, including my own. I hate the fact that I seek comfort in the bottle. I grab a few more bottles and repeat the process of taking the drink to the head. I don't know which drink causes me to fall asleep, but all I do know is that the sun is my alarm clock. The bright beams once again peek through the curtains and cause me to get up. I stagger out of bed and close the blinds.

I then fall face first back onto the bed and go to sleep. I don't have any appointments schedule for today so that will give me time to recover. Besides, I can't go around church folks smelling like a bar.

It isn't long before there is a knock on the door. I stagger out of bed and head toward the door but the knocks feel like sledgehammers hitting the door.

"I'm coming! Hold on!"

I open the door and Spider is on the other side. I thank God that I am not a criminal because Spider's stature is quite imposing.

"We need to talk." Spider does not wait for an invitation. He uses his girth to force his way into the room.

"Okay, come on in." I close the door with one eye still squinting. Spider has already helped himself to one of my cigarettes on the table.

"So what's up?" I ask.

"I can't find your boy." Spider lets out a trail of smoke from the cigarette.

"What?" I ask.

Spider gets up and starts to pace the floor. That is the last thing that I expect to come out of his mouth. One time Spider found a man who hid himself underneath a tree trunk. There was another time when Spider found a ninety-pound woman, suspected of murder, hidden in the air vents of her job. Spider's success is that he looks in places that most police officers would not suspect someone to hide in. To get a lock on Tony Robinson does not seem that hard of a task for someone like Spider.

"What happened?" I ask.

"I've checked all over and there's not a trace of him. At least nothing that's within a week ago. He's gone man."

This is an unfortunate turn of events. The last thing I need is for Spider to be unsuccessful in his mission. "Are you sure you can't find him? Maybe he left town like what we originally thought."

"If he had left town, I would've known. I've checked everywhere: bus stations, train stations, airports, and rental cars. Nothing! I checked with close family, friends, and coaches and no one has seen or heard from him for at least the last week."

I don't mean to question Spider's skills but I am trying to wrap my brain around the fact that an average Joe slipped through the fingers of a skilled recovery agent.

"There's something we need to start considering, Nic."

"What's that?" I ask.

"That your boy may have been murked."

It seems like my heart forgets to beat for a full minute. I am familiar with the urban term "murk." Spider means that the first gentleman might have been murdered.

Chapter Thirteen

Murder! The word alone chills my blood. *The first gentleman couldn't have been murdered.* I have worked a lot of cases and I have found myself in a lot of odd situations, but never have I encountered a murder. I have no intentions of getting mixed up in a murder. There has to be another reason why no one has either seen nor heard from Tony Robinson in over a week.

"You can't be serious," I say to Spider.

"I wish I wasn't but no one disappears for two weeks without leaving town, and I can't find him." Spider paces the floor and flicks ash from the cigarette as he paces.

"I met with Pastor Robinson yesterday and she said that there had been no activity made on their bank accounts," I say.

"Correction—no one disappears for two weeks without leaving town or withdrawing any money from their bank accounts."

"This can't be happening." I start to pace the floor and, as a result, I grab a cigarette and light it.

"I know it sounds farfetched, but in my line of work the only people with no activity are the ones who have been buried six feet under. The ones in hiding are constantly moving and that's what creates a trail, but your boy's trail turns cold after a week."

"There has to be another reason."

"There's not," Spider replies.

"There has to be, Spider! Don't tell me that a pastor's husband has been murdered. That doesn't make sense. What secrets could she possibly have that would cause someone to end Tony's life? end Tony's life?"

"People have done more for less."

Spider is right. I hate that he is right, but Spider is right. Tony Robinson's activity has been strange and his disappearance has been even stranger. The fact that he has not used any of his bank accounts or credit cards is even stranger. It just doesn't add up.

"What was this guy involved in?" Spider asks.

"Nothing. Everything I had on him I gave to you. He's a software engineer and the first gentleman of the church."

Spider finally takes a seat down in the chair and I sit down on the edge of the bed. This information is heavy and I know that there is something that Spider and I have overlooked, but I can't put my finger on it.

"Is it possible that he had a gambling addiction or drug habit?" Spider asks.

"No. I would've known and his wife would've told me. We need to take a step back and look at this situation in a different light. Tony obviously doesn't want to be found, so the immediate circle of family and friends are out. There must be someone else he trusts and knows he could turn to for help in a situation like this."

Spider scratches his goatee and I scratch the back of my head. My information on Tony and his list of contacts is pretty expansive. I am certain that someone would've seen him within the last two days, but Spider has nothing, and the theory that foul play is at work seems a lot more viable.

"So what do you want me to do now?" Spider asks.

I stand up and Spider stands up at the same time. "Wait. I'm headed to the church to see what more I can dig up. I'll call you when I got something, but for now, wait."

"All right. I got you."

I drive to the church with my original plan being severely derailed. I had plans to go to the church and meet up with Spider later to track down the first gentleman's whereabouts. I had no idea that Spider would appear and tell me that he can't find Tony Robinson. So when I arrive at the church I make a beeline to Pastor Robinson's office.

I knock on the door and Minister Blackwell opens the door. Pastor Robinson is there going over her documents.

"We need to talk." I look at Minister Blackwell. "Alone."

"Give us a minute," Pastor Robinson says to Minister Blackwell. Minister Blackwell takes his leave. I help close the door behind Minister Blackwell.

"What seems to be going on, Minister Dungy?"

"My guy can't find your husband."

"I thought you said he could find anything."

"He can, which leads him to believe that your husband might've been murdered."

That sparks the first semblance of emotions from Pastor Robinson. "Murder!"

"I'm glad that I have your attention. If your husband has been murdered that means you got a lot more problems to worry about than your husband not showing up to church."

The news of Tony Robinson's possible death has caused Pastor Robinson to get out of her chair and pace the floor. "Lord Jesus! Lord, please don't put that on me."

I just want to rattle Pastor Robinson's cage and get her to be more involved in providing useful information. I had long suspected that there is something that Pastor Robinson is hiding. I now have my doubts.

"I need to know who was having an affair and if there have been any threats made on either of you."

"No one cheated that I know of and the only threats I receive are the ones that state that I'm going to hell for being a woman preacher."

I turn around and I head toward the door. I don't have time for games. I can walk and pocket the money that I already made from this job.

"I didn't cheat on my husband, but my husband did cheat on me. At least I think he has!"

That last statement stops me dead in my tracks. "How do you know?" I ask with my back still turned.

"A wife always knows when she's lost her husband. It's just up to her whether she wants to admit it."

I roll my eyes because I don't need a Lifetime Movie Network soliloquy. "Who?" I ask.

"I don't know for sure."

"Then give me an educated guess."

"Sister Deborah. She's known as Ms. Fast Panties throughout the church and she used to flirt with my husband just to spite me."

"Did she succeed?"

"Sometimes. I'm only human."

"Did she enrage you to the point where you felt like doing something? You felt like taking it out on your husband?"

"Why would you ask me that?"

"Because you have a missing husband, $150,000 from an unknown source, and more questions than answers."

Pastor Robinson makes a choking gesture with her hands and then clasps them together like she is about to pray. "What does it matter how you got paid? The check cleared and you took the job. Now do your job! Find my husband!" Pastor Robinson slams her hand down on the desk and keeps it there to hold herself up. The news that the man she loves may never return home, I can imagine, is more than unsettling. "Oh, God, Lord, please bring my husband back to me."

It is as if I have left the room. Pastor Robinson starts pacing the floor. She is beside herself and I have to suspend the hardball questions for a moment to get more information on Ms. Fast Panties.

"Why do you suspect your husband is having an affair with this woman? Why haven't you asked him about her?"

"I don't know. Because I had too much pride to ask. I don't want to sound weak or insecure."

"Pride goes before a fall, and right now your ministry is falling," I say.

I am perplexed and do not know what to do, but I need to pick up the cold trail so Spider can find where Pastor Robinson's husband is hiding.

"You have to find him. You have to; I can't help people if my life is jacked up."

"I'm going to take your word for it that you didn't cheat on your husband, but there is something between you and your husband that you're not telling me. It shouldn't take the possibility of your husband being murdered for you to care all of a sudden. We got a tough road ahead and that's after I find your husband."

"If you were married would you ask your wife to give up her dream? That's what Tony asked of me every day. Every day he told me that I had no business being on that pulpit. Now we put on a good show in front of the congregation, but he was anything but a supporting husband."

"First things first, Pastor. First we find your husband, and then we work on your marriage."

I am sure that if I can get the Robinsons in a room together then I can get them to reconcile. Pastor Robinson seems willing to overlook the affair and it is just a matter of convincing Tony that his wife did not have an affair.

"Bible Study is tonight."

That statement comes out of left field. Who is teaching tonight's Bible Study is the last thing on my mind.

"Yes. Minister Blackwell is supposed to teach," I say.

"I think you should teach," Pastor Robinson says.

I don't know what shocks me more: Pastor Robinson making a suggestion; or that Pastor Robinson's suggestion is that I teach tonight's Bible Study.

"Whoa, whoa, whoa! I haven't taught a Bible Study since the Clinton administration."

"But you are, among other things, an ordained minister. People are starting to ask questions regarding your appearance, and Sister Deborah would be interested in you."

"Listen, I can get what I need to get from Sister Deborah without having to get up on the pulpit."

"Correct me if I'm wrong but aren't you a minister?"

Standing in front of Pastor Robinson I realize that she is the only real minister in the room and that is a hard pill to swallow. I traded my calling for secrets and money. I have gone far off the path that I originally wanted to go. I know I am a Christian, though not a good one. I know that I love God, but I have a level of disdain for His people, so, no, I am not a minister, I am a cover-up artist.

"Yes, I am. I am a minister," I lie.

"Then you should be ready to answer the call when the call is made. And I would think that you would want to be done with this job as fast as possible."

I hate to admit it, but Pastor Robinson has a point. I need to get close to Sister Deborah to find out what she knows. "So what is tonight's Bible Study about?"

"Grace and mercy," Pastor Robinson says.

Grace and mercy, that's what I will need to get through tonight's Bible Study.

"I'll do it. I'll teach tonight's class."

***

I sit in an available office and pore over the scriptures. I sweat up a storm. My taste buds crave a cigarette and a drink. I have no problems functioning in my original capacity as a Mr. Fix-it. I can walk into a roomful of power players and tell them where to go and what to do without blinking, but a simple Bible Study lesson has me sweating like a high school student about to take the SATs.

Strange how it's been twenty years since my ordination and I am just now using my title for its original purpose. I remember a time when all I wanted to do on a Tuesday or a Wednesday was study the Bible and prepare a Bible Study lesson. That is, until I realized that ministry is not about being able to get up and perform.

Most people see a T.D. Jakes, Creflo Dollar, or a Billy Graham and they think that it's easy to preach the Word. The truth about ministry is that it requires one to get their hands dirty. It requires someone to look into the muck and be willing to put their hands into the muck to save a life. I found that out a little too late.

A knock on the door disrupts my flow and derails my thought process.

"Come on in," I say without looking up from my notes.

The door opens and Minister Blackwell enters the room. "It's about that time. You'll go up after Kanisha leads praise and worship."

"Who?" I ask.

"One of Pastor's projects. She's real special. Pastor Robinson lets her lead praise and worship on some of the Bible Studies."

Under normal circumstances I would care to explore more details regarding this Kanisha character, but I have work to do. I place the legal-size note tablet in the middle of my Bible and close it. I get up and follow Minister Blackwell out of the office and into the lobby. I pass by the same greeter from the other night with the infectious smile.

"Good evening. God Bless you!" the greeter says.

I stop and pivot toward the woman. "God bless you; and what's your name, sister?"

"Victory! Victory Morgan." Victory extends her hand and I shake it. I feel a nudge in my back and realize that it is Minister Blackwell urging me on.

"This way, Minister Dungy," Minister Blackwell says.

Despite my reluctance, I follow Minister Blackwell into the sanctuary. I enter the sanctuary like a heavyweight boxer heading to a title fight. I have on the same collar shirt I wore earlier. I didn't have time to change. I enter the sanctuary and Kanisha is leading a small group in a Gospel rap.

"Say OWW. Give it up for Jesus!" Kanisha says before she starts rapping.

I understand why Minister Blackwell referred to Kanisha as special. I take a seat next to Pastor Robinson and observe this buffoonery. Kanisha's appearance tells an exhaustive story. She has tattoos all over her body from her neck down. Most of her tattoos are carefully hidden. My hair is both longer and less vibrant than Kanisha's honey blond hair. I would've figured her to be a lesbian back in the day, but today's youth does some of the strangest things that I can't begin to explain. The song concludes and Kanisha takes a moment to catch her breath.

"I just wanted to give an honor to God and my Lord and Savior Jesus Christ for saving me and bringing me a mighty long ways. I know that without Him I'm nothing and I want to thank God for our pastor, Pastor Robinson." Kanisha is still out of breath. "If it wasn't for her speaking and pouring into my life, God knows where I would be. So thank you, Pastor Robinson, for not judging me, and thank you, Jesus, for sending this awesome woman into my life. I love you and I want to be like you when I grow up," Kanisha says.

After Kanisha sits down in her seat, Minister Blackwell gets up and approaches the pulpit.

"Praise the Lord. Praise the Lord. Praise the Lord!" Minister Blackwell says.

The congregation gives Minister Blackwell a halfhearted response. I imagine that most of the people who attend Bible Study desperately need something to get them through the week. Sunday morning does an excellent job of inspiring people on Sunday, but it's easy to stay inspired when all that follows is a hefty meal, football, long naps, and evening programs. I find that it is hard for a Christian to stay inspired once Monday morning hits. Tuesday night Bible Study is a way for the saints to recharge in order to go back into a secular environment.

"We have a special treat tonight, and our pastor has been extremely gracious to allow Minister Nicodemus Dungy from Southern California to speak with us tonight. Jubilee, let's give a warm welcome to Minister Dungy and let's tell him to preach!"

"Preach!" the congregation says.

"Amen and God bless!" Minister Blackwell says.

Minister Blackwell invites me up and I walk up to the pulpit. I feel awkward standing in the pulpit. I never care for standing over people and shouting down scriptures. I decide to walk down the steps and stand in front of the congregation.

"What is grace? Grace is not just the ability to overcome sin. God has given us the grace to be overcomers. Grace is not the excuse to sin, but the power to transcend your life."

I feel like a complete hypocrite. I use my grace to sin and indulge. I stopped feeling empowered a long time ago, and one thing is for sure, a congregation knows when the preacher doesn't believe in what they are preaching.

"The Apostle Paul talks about how those who are delivered from sin do not have to continue in it."

I get a few amens, but most of them are silent. I now have a newfound respect for Pastor McMurray. Getting up in front of a crowd is not easy.

"Grace is not just there to catch you when you fall. It's there to pick you up and remind you who you are."

"Jesus!" a woman says in the back.

I feel a rush of adrenaline as the amens start to pour in. I turn to Pastor Robinson and she is mentally someplace else. A tidal wave of emotions overtake me. I look down at one of my scriptural references and several other scriptures will pop up. Examples that can further illustrate my point also come in like a tidal wave.

"The world would have us think that 'grace' is a term reserved for the weak, but we as Christians know, that grace gives us the power to stand. When we get down on our knees to seek God for help, God extends His hand and helps us to our feet."

The amens become thunderous and people start to stand up and give praises to God. I close my eyes and take in the moment. My skin breaks out in bumps and even a smile creeps out of my face. I have let the circumstances of life and my profession beat me to my knees, but at this very moment I feel like God has just helped me to my feet. This is supposed to be a Bible Study and not a sermon, but I cannot ignore what everything in my spirit is telling me.

I look back at Pastor Robinson and she is not even paying attention. The concern for her husband has finally resonated with Pastor Robinson. I need to find her husband and find him fast before Pastor Robinson self-destructs.

After services conclude, I stay back to chat with some of the members. Well, at least I give off the illusion that I want to chat with other members. I really want to talk to Sister Deborah. And I'm not disappointed; Sister Deborah approaches me as predicted by Pastor Robinson.

"God bless you. I'm Sister Deborah. That was an awesome sermon," Sister Deborah says.

"Thank you very much, Sister Deborah. I had to let the Holy Spirit have its way."

"I see; tell me, Minister Dungy, are you going back to Southern California anytime soon?"

"No, not anytime soon."

Sister Deborah's face lights up at my statement. Sister Deborah is a caramel-complexioned beauty with full lips and more curves than a race track.

"Well then, I might have to have you over for dinner."

And Pastor Robinson is right; Sister Deborah buys it hook, line and sinker. I, on the other hand, will get more than what I bargain for.

Chapter Fourteen

After Bible Study I am on an emotional high. I feel like for the first time in a long time I have made a connection with the people. I don't get the dirty feeling I get when I work behind the scenes. Tonight I feel like a real minister of the Gospel. I celebrate tonight by picking up some Chinese takeout and going back to my hotel room.

I have a pack of cigarettes that I have not opened yet. I even have a bottle of Crown Royal that has not been touched in the last few days. I decide to wet my taste buds with a lime-flavored soda that I bought along with the Chinese food. I am halfway through my sweet and sour chicken when the phone rings. I think it is Spider, who I am going to meet up with later, but lo and behold it is Sister Deborah.

I have given her the cell phone number to my disposable phone. Hardly anyone has my real phone number, outside of my clients, my few friends, and closest family members. When I am done with a job I want every piece of evidence that I was in town to be able to fit in a trash bag, and a cell phone is one of them.

It is 11:47 P.M. Something tells me that Sister Deborah is not calling for prayer.

"Hello, Sister Deborah. How are you?"

"Terrible. I made too much red velvet cake and I have no one to share it with. I was thinking that I could drop it off to you at your hotel?"

Something tells me that she is offering more than just a piece of cake. "That's really thoughtful, Sister Deborah, but my hotel room is a mess."

For one, I don't let anyone except for my client know where I stay. For two, I need to get to Sister Deborah's apartment to see if there is evidence of an affair between her and First Gentleman Tony Robinson. I also need to see if Tony has been by her house recently.

"Well, you can come over if you like."

"Well, I wouldn't want to inconvenience you," I say.

"The pleasure would be all mines."

Too easy. "Okay, I'll see you in a bit."

When I arrive at Sister Deborah's house she opens the door in a royal blue nightgown that reveals neither too much nor too little.

"I'm sorry, I fell asleep. I didn't think you were going to show up."

It only took me twenty minutes from the time she called to arrive to her house.

"I could come back tomorrow if you like." I pivot to act like I am going to leave, and she stops me gently with her hands.

"Don't be silly; come on in."

She leads me in and I do not put up much of a resistance. I enter her living room, which is fit for a Realtor to show. For a woman like Sister Deborah, who is known for entertaining company, white furniture and white carpet without a spot or blemish is impressive. As promised, she has some red velvet cake on the clear glass coffee table along with something extra. There is an open bottle of Moscato next to two wine glasses. One of the glasses has ruby red lipstick on it and is half full. The other glass has not been touched.

"I have a nice Moscato to wash down the cake with."

I am not a big wine drinker. Something about alcohol with fruit flavor cheapens the experience for me. "No, thank you, but I would like to go ahead and have a piece of your delicious cake."

I sit down at a safe distance and observe the living room, in search of clues. "This is a really nice place you have."

"Thank you. I've mastered the art of finding the best deal; unfortunately, most of my furniture was purchased at a yard sale. There were a lot of yard sales after the bubble burst on the dot-com companies."

Desperate times bring forth desperate measures and desperate times also bring forth desperate people.

"I have a nice office and a wonderful bedroom as a result."

I need to dictate the flow of the conversation. "I would love to get a tour."

"Well, come on." Sister Deborah gets up and takes me by the hand. I follow her to the back of the house, where her office is located. I make sure to take mental photographs of everything, and notice something different about the office carpet from the living room. While the living room carpet is spotless, this carpet has a little bit of a scuff mark. I can tell that the scuff mark is a boot print.

Sister Deborah doesn't have to worry about entertaining company in her office, so she probably overlooked the mark or doesn't realize it is there. But I notice that the mark is about the size of a twelve shoe, which means that the guy has a big foot and is at least six feet tall. He may be over 200 pounds. This is all speculation, but the prospect that the boot runs the same size as Tony Robinson's foot is a good step in the right direction; no pun intended. In the midst of the photos I notice that there are no pictures of a husband or children, just family and pictures of church events. One picture involves Sister Deborah with First Gentleman Tony Robinson. The picture is innocent enough, but I am not here to play nice. I am here to kick up dust.

"So are you and first gentleman really close?" I ask.

"No more than normal."

"Where is he? I haven't seen him."

"I don't know." Sister Deborah shrugs her shoulders and takes the picture from me. Sister Deborah places the picture back on her desk.

I scan the room and don't see any other evidence, which means I need to check out her other rooms and need to fast-track this tour. "Any idea why he would just up and disappear?" I ask.

"There are lots of reasons for a man to up and leave his wife, but the best person to ask questions of would be his wife."

Sister Deborah's tone indicates that she is envious of Pastor Robinson and Tony Robinson's marriage. How does that saying go? "Always a bride . . ." Anyway, Sister Deborah is starting to show her true colors. I need to dig a little more, but still I need to be careful.

"What about you? Was marriage ever in the picture?" I ask.

"Of course, but if a man isn't coming correct, then why should I settle? I have exquisite taste and I'm not ashamed of it."

Sister Deborah gives me a look so seductive that it comes with its own gravitational pull. Sister Deborah shifts her body so that I can get a good look at her silhouette. I may be a man of God, but I am still a man and a man with needs. For the most part my work keeps me busy and active enough to the point where I don't have to worry about those needs. Sister Deborah's body reminds me of those needs, and I am in a vulnerable state.

I pretend to look at my watch. "Well, look at the time. I got to go."

"No!" Sister Deborah takes me by the hand. "Please stay. There is something I wanted you to see."

She leads me into her bedroom and her eggshell white carpet is replaced with royal blue, but there is an imprint almost identical to that on the office carpet, which makes a deep impact.

I am now certain that the individual is a man and he weighs over 200 pounds. The scent in the room is stronger. That means that the individual was here earlier and Sister Deborah probably wants to cover up the masculine scent. This may be conjecture or speculation but Sister Deborah really does have a large appetite. The question is, who is the guy she just dined on?

Chapter Fifteen

"Must you fulfill every movie stereotype?" I'm referring to the fact that I'm in a parked car; on the passenger side of Spider's Chevy Impala. Spider also has an assortment of donuts in his car. I grab a chocolate doughnut with sprinkles and finish it in three bites. With the tinted windows, I am certain that no one will spot me, especially Sister Deborah, who I am certain will not speak to me after I left her place to avoid being caught up in my own personal drama. I have many vices, but promiscuity is not one of them. Have I had a slipup here and there? Yes. I'm not proud of what I have done, but I have learned that single acts can be devastating, but a bad habit is guaranteed to be destructive. From my experience I have witnessed great men fall from high pedestals on account of a relationship. Sex, drugs, and alcohol is a recipe for destruction and I draw the line with my drinking problem and cigarette addiction.

"This is pointless. I don't know why we're even here." I adjust my seat for more comfort. I rub the back of my head out of frustration. This case is really starting to get away from me.

"We're here because you think the pastor's husband is tapping the church whore."

"That's right."

"It would be easier if he was a fugitive." Spider checks his rearview window.

"How so?"

"Because most people don't want to harbor a fugitive because they don't want to go to jail; but hiding a guy from his wife, people are little bit more inclined to help a brother out."

"Since when did you become a romantic?" I ask.

"Never. Since when did you become a cynic?"

"When I started working in ministry."

"I don't know many preachers who would sit in a parked car outside of someone's house. They mostly do their work from pulpits."

"This is where the real work begins . . . I feel like this was not exactly what I was called to do, but this was what I was meant to do. What about you?"

"You mean was I always meant to be a bounty hunter?" Spider puts his head back and chuckles. "I don't know. I've always known I was meant to be a protector of some kind. Just like how you were meant to help people."

"I don't know about that," I say.

I am certain the list of careers I have ruined exceeds the number of careers I helped. It is rare when I feel like I am a minister. It is not until moments like last night that I feel like I am a true minister of the Gospel.

"You still think our guy might've been murdered?" I ask.

"I don't know. I think I was just being paranoid. Then again, maybe I'm just losing my touch. Maybe it's time for me to do something else."

"I hear you, but I don't think there's anything else guys like us could do. I mean, you could do something else, but I don't think anything else would make you feel alive. This is it, this is your thing!"

Spider chuckles to himself, and though I'm not a mind reader, I know why he laughs. Spider knows that I am right. There's a fine line between what we can do and what we're meant to do. Spider understands that line and he also understands where he stands in the grand scheme of things.

"So I guess its God's will for me to spend my life looking down dark alleys and corners for criminals."

"Someone has to have the courage to do it," I say.

That is the last thing I say to Spider before we spend the next ten minutes in complete silence. I drift off to sleep until Spider gives me a tap on my shoulder. I open my eyes and I see a dark figure creep up the driveway of Sister Deborah's house.

"Here we go," I say.

I can't make out the image until the figure steps into the light outside of Sister Deborah's front door. The guy is around my age with a salt-and-pepper goatee and hair as black as coal. Tony Robinson is light skinned, which means that I have not found the first gentleman. This guy is yet another one of Sister Deborah's suitors.

"Let's go, Spider; he's not coming home."

Spider does not hesitate to turn on the engine of his Impala and pull away. The Impala disappears in the night as we leave Sister Deborah's house.

"That was a waste," I say.

"Not really, because we now have an idea of where the husband might've been. I'll follow up later at this spot and see if he comes by."

Spider drops me off at the hotel and I go into my room with every intention of smoking a cigarette with a glass of Crown Royal. I first go over to the TV and turn it on. I last left the TV on the news.

"Breaking news; we now take it out to Laura Cruz," a male newscaster says.

"Thank you, Jim," the on-the-scene reporter says. "I'm on the corner of Ridgemount Avenue and Jefferson Boulevard. Police have just discovered in a Dumpster a body that was rolled up in carpet."

I shake my head at the sight. Some people can be complete monsters. A closer inspection and I realize that this murder occurred in a familiar area. My heart forgets to beat at the sight of the news. Where the police have found the body is in the exact same neighborhood where Sister Deborah lives. If Sister Deborah and Tony Robinson were having an affair, then that leaves me to wonder about the identity of the victim.

Chapter Sixteen

I get back to Sister Deborah's house in less time than I did before. The only issue is that this sleepy neighborhood is ablaze with yellow caution tape and sirens from police squad cars and ambulances. Neighbors are outside of their homes and they are not concerned with their attire. I am concerned with the safety of Sister Deborah and the identity of the victim. I'm not a humanitarian, but I don't wish something bad to happen to anyone, especially someone being brutally murdered.

The police interview some of the witnesses while the medical examiners work the crime scene and they tag the different pieces of material. I thought about being a medical examiner at one point. I felt like that was the closest I could come to being a detective without being shot at, but medical examiners go to school too long for my taste and rack up too many student loans.

The body has a sheet over it and I know that the body will not be moved anytime soon. I can tell that the victim is not a small guy, which means the murderer is either a big guy or the murderer has not operated alone. A chill sweeps over my entire body. Spider and I left Sister Deborah's house less than an hour ago, and that means that if the murderer dumped the body, then it was within that hour. Then again, the body could've been dumped earlier and I didn't know it.

Sister Deborah's neighborhood is real quiet and you can tell that the people in the community go about their business and do not bother anyone. The murderer could've dropped the body anywhere, but chose here to send a message to this quiet area. Either that or the victim has ties to this community.

I see Sister Deborah in front of her house with a pink bathrobe on. She has a man who is head and shoulders taller than her. He resembles the man Spider and I saw earlier tonight. The man rubs her shoulders and Sister Deborah proves to be a woman who is adaptable. I don't know what possess me to go over to her, but I want to check to make sure she is okay. I maneuver through the crowd that stood still like zombies. Once I am in Sister Deborah's sight, she smacks her lips at me.

"I know you don't have the nerves to come up here after you just up and left!" Sister Deborah says, and the guy she is with pivots from around her and sizes me up.

In a fair fight the guy would take me, but I don't fight fair. I fight to win, and please believe that I wouldn't hesitate to kick him in the jewels if I had to.

"I just wanted to see if you were okay," I say.

"I was worried about you. I thought something happened to you," Sister Deborah says.

"Oh please, put away the violin will you? That doesn't suit you," I say and the guy takes a step closer to me. "Don't try it!"

The guy heeds my threat and loses respect from Sister Deborah in the process. "Whatever! All I know is that you ain't no Apostle Paul."

"And you ain't Esther either." I rub the back of my head because I don't know what else to do. "Look, I saw the news and I came by to see if you were okay. It's clear that you are, so have a nice night." That is all I say before I leave. I don't have time to squabble with a promiscuous woman; I have a first gentleman to find.

***

From the crime scene I go to Spider's house. Spider manages to eke out a living that affords him a two-bedroom flat in the heart of Rancho Cordova. Rancho Cordova is a city about twenty miles outside of Sacramento. I am greeted by Chopper, Spider's black and tan coonhound. Chopper doesn't take his eyes off me until Spider arrives at the door.

"Come here, Chopper," Spider says with a whistle, and Chopper goes inside the house and takes a seat next to his master.

"Guinness!" I hold up the six pack of beer.

"Aww, dog, I gave up drinking a year ago."

I feel bad. The last thing that I want is to challenge Spider's sobriety. The scripture talks about not causing your brother to stumble. "I'm sorry."

"Don't worry about it. I have friends who come over to watch the football games and they drink Guinness."

I walk into Spider's living room and drop my jacket over Spider's loveseat. Spider's living room consists of hardwood floors and his desk is stacked with empty pizza boxes. Spider's wall looks like an ongoing saga. The wall is full of maps and most-wanted posters. To glance at this wall is unnerving, but for Spider I can imagine that he gets fuel from the hunt.

"Any word?" I ask.

"Not yet. They haven't confirmed the victim's identity, but I'm pretty sure that it's not your boy."

Somehow, Spider's words do not provide comfort. It is a long shot that the victim is Tony Robinson, but it is not outside of the realm of possibility that it is Tony. I can't shake that small percentage in me that thinks Tony Robinson has been murdered.

"Let's just entertain the idea that it is the guy we are looking for. Why would anyone want to kill him?"

"I don't know. The further I go into this case the less sense it makes. Maybe he was involved with the wrong woman and it's a crime of passion."

"Possibly. I went by Sister Deborah's place and she seemed just as shocked by the murder as anybody. I'll rule her out as a possible suspect."

"Was this guy involved in some illegal activity?"

"I can't imagine the first gentleman being involved in anything that would cause him to be murdered and thrown in a Dumpster. Did you encounter anything with his friends? Did anyone mention his habits or anything of that nature? Any vices?"

"Nothing. Your boy lived a pretty pious lifestyle." Spider sits back in his chair.

Spider gets up and makes his way toward his computer. I follow Spider to the computer and stand over him. Spider clicks on his mouse and gets rid of the Sofia Vergara screensaver. His computer now has the Google Maps page up. Spider zooms in on a particular area of Sacramento.

"I've covered this whole area." Spider draws a circle with his finger. "From friends to family to coworkers, no one has seen or heard from Tony in a week; and you said his wife hasn't seen him in over two weeks."

"But when I was approached by the situation, Tony had already been gone for a week so that means his wife was not the last person to see him," I say.

"I checked all of the hotels around in the area and there was no record of Tony staying at any place in the area," Spider says.

"Maybe he stayed under an assumed name or under someone else's name."

"If he did, then it wasn't anyone from his inner circle," Spider replies.

I put my hands in my pockets and start to pace the floor. Even though I know it's a long shot regarding Tony being a victim of a brutal murder, outside of that theory, I got nothing.

"What about this murder?" I ask.

"Without knowing the details I think the position of the body was planted there to send a message."

"A message to whom?" I wonder.

Spider shrugs his shoulders while looking at the maps. "I don't know, but there's one type of murderer who does their killings with a specific agenda in mind."

"A serial killer," Spider and I say in unison.

Just saying it out loud feels like a knife in my chest. "Offhand what do we know about serial killers?"

Spider turns around and gets off of his chair. He walks over to the dry-erase board he has on the wall next to his maps and most-wanted posters. Spider erases what was on his board with the sleeve of his thermal shirt and starts to write on the board with a black marker.

"We know that ninety percent are men." Spider writes the word "male" on the board.

"We know most come from broken, single-parent homes. Either that or they have abusive fathers," I reply.

"They're usually social outcasts and have high IQs." Spider writes his comments and my comments on the board.

"I got a friend who works for the *Times*. I wonder if he can shed some light on the subject." Since I don't have anything to go on, I might as well consider all avenues.

I pick up my cell and call my buddy from the *L.A. Times,* Paul. I haven't spoken to Paul since the day he brought me the news that Pastor Lewis had committed suicide.

"Hello?" Paul asks.

"Hey, Paul, this is Nic. Listen, have you seen the news about a murder in Sacramento?"

"Yeah, I've heard about it. Why? Where are you now?" Paul asks.

"I'm in Sac."

"What a surprise. What are you doing in Sac?"

"I'm doing some work for a church."

"I bet," Paul says.

The last time I talked to Paul, he delivered the news that Pastor Lewis committed suicide. A very sore subject.

"Hey Paul, I was wondering if you heard anything about the murders going on up here?"

"I have and , I am on my way up there. I was wondering if you could pick me up?" Paul asks.

"Sure!" And just like that, the call ends. There must be something to this murder to cause my friend to come up from Los Angeles.

"What's up?" Spider asks.

"We need to pick my friend up from the airport."

We arrive outside of the arrival station at the Sacramento airport. The airport, which is usually subdued, is vibrant, which means that there are several reporters coming in to get the story of the hacked-up victim. My friend finally emerges with his signature black leather jacket and tie. I chuckle to myself; my friend wears a leather jacket because he thinks he is cool.

"Funny finding you here," Paul says as he enters the car.

"I'm here on church business."

"Sure, and I'm here to interview the Pope." Paul takes a moment to size up Spider before he sets his attention back on me. "Who's he?" Paul asks.

"Spider. I'm a bounty hunter," he answers for himself.
"You keep some interesting friends," Paul says.
"So why are you here?" I ask Paul.

There had to be more to this murder for Paul to make
a sudden trip up North. Sadly there is no shortage of
murder cases in Los Angeles.

"I'm here to do a story on the body found in the dumpster."

For as long as I've known my friend, Paul has always
wanted to win a Pulitzer. I know that there has to be more
to this than he is saying.

"So what is going on with the case?" I ask.

"I'm not telling you. This is sensitive information,"
Paul replies.

"We can help?"

"He can help." Paul points to Spider. "You, on the other
hand, what are you going to do? Pray and lay hands on
the sick?"

"I have some information that may be helpful."

Paul carries on an internal debate, I can tell. He then
waits and pauses for a moment. "Okay, but tell me this:
what do you know about the Husband Stalker?"

It takes me a moment to remember that the Husband
Stalker was a serial killer who went around murdering
married men.

"What about him?" I ask.

"We think he's back!" Paul says.

I shudder to think that Tony Robinson might've been
the Husband Stalker's latest victim.

Chapter Seventeen

In the early nineties there was a rash of serial killings that caused men to run to their homes and hide. At first the news reported the murders as random killings, but later on they saw a common link with the victims. All victims had wives who were in a position of authority. The husbands took on nontraditional roles from alpha males, and as a result they were targeted and killed by one lone suspect known as the Husband Stalker.

The male victims were mutilated in areas I bother not to imagine. I got chills while I read through the articles online. I remember being in a debate about the stalker in my criminal psychology course and I long held the belief that the killer came from a broken home where he saw his father in an emasculate role.

The last victim that we are aware of was a stay-at-home father whose wife was an appellate court judge. After that, the stalker disappeared and was not heard from for years. Now, is it possible that the Stalker might've resurfaced?

I hope that the stalker has not resurfaced and that Tony Robinson was not one of his latest victims. What are the chances that the stalker has, in fact, resurfaced and that my guy was his latest victim?

After we pick Paul up from the airport we go right back to Spider's place to try to figure this whole murder scenario out.

"Wow? You guys have already got started," Paul says as he admires Spider's board.

Spider stands next to his dry-erase board, which is full, with the exception of one thin corner. "Now that we believe it may be the Husband Stalker, let's establish what we know about his movements."

"We know that the first string of murders took place in San Jose," Paul says.

Spider writes "San Jose" on the board and then goes over to his maps. "The last victim was found on the side of the road next to the 101 freeway."

"That makes sense," I say.

"How so?" Paul asks.

"The 101 is a major freeway that goes along California. He could be anywhere between San Jose and Santa Barbara before the police even found the body."

Paul shrugs his shoulders in agreement and Spiders writes "the 101 freeway" on the board. "That means when things start to get too hot, look for his last victim to appear near a major freeway."

"The 80," we all say in chorus.

"He can end up in Reno before we even know it," I say.

"Any ideas who the victim might be?" Paul asks.

"We've been looking into a missing minister's husband," Spider says.

I don't want Spider to divulge such information. Paul pounces on such newsworthy gossip. "Yeah, but I don't think the guy I'm looking for could be the victim. His wife is not a popular figure."

"I wouldn't rule it out. A minister is traditionally a man's role, so a husband to a woman minister fits the Husband Stalker's mode even if the woman isn't that popular."

"Even so, I doubt that it's my guy," I say with my hands in my pockets.

"So you're looking for a missing husband, Nic?"

"Just trying to help resolve a marital spat."

Paul lets out a sadistic laugh because he knows that nothing with me is ever simple. "Well, gentlemen, this is all fascinating, but I need to get to my hotel room and unpack. We'll compare notes tomorrow. Nic, can you give me a ride?"

"Sure," I say to Paul and then I give Spider a head nod. "Tomorrow then."

I pray that by tomorrow I can cancel this meeting because Tony Robinson will somehow reappear.

I need a drink. A drink will be good right now and a drink is right in front of me. I grab the bottle by the neck and twist the cap. I inhale the strong scent of the alcohol and allow it to tickle my nose. I want to drink, but I don't need to drink. The choice is simple; it comes down to wants and needs.

It is a simple decision but so hard to make. I go to the sink and I start to pour out the contents in the sink. I know I will rejoice for not giving into temptation, but I will be upset with ruining a perfectly good bottle of cognac.

There's a knock on the door and I open it without considering the fact that I have a bottle of alcohol in my hands.

"Minister Dungy." Minister Blackwell can't take his eyes off of the bottle.

"It's not what you think. What's up?"

"I've been leaving you messages and you haven't been returning calls. I thought something had happened to you."

That much is true. Since the recent turn of events I have screened all of my calls and have not checked in with the church. "I've been really busy. Why? What's up?"

"We needed you to preach tonight."

"Oh no! I'm in no condition to preach."

Minister Blackwell focuses on the bottle. I focus on the minister and not on my bottle.

"Not that, I've been good, but I'm following up on a lead. I need to meet up with my guy and see if he has any more intel on Tony Robinson."

"It's our Friday night service and unless you're going to let Pastor preach, then you're the best man for the job."

I have not showered yet today. I still smell like yesterday, but despite my brain being cloudy I know that I should go. I need to go and get out of my hotel room.

"Give me ten minutes," I say as I swing the door open long enough for Minister Blackwell to catch it and enter.

I hop in the shower, and after about three minutes I am out. I'm sure the shower misses me. I dry off and throw on some clothes. As I have foretold, in ten minutes I am out the door with Minister Blackwell and my Bible.

"Should I be concerned?" Minister Blackwell asks.

I cannot afford to play coy or stupid. I know what the minister is referring to; he is referring to seeing a minister of the Gospel open the door with a bottle of cognac in his hands.

"No, not at all. My internal issues will not prevent me from performing my duties to the best of my abilities."

"But isn't it a contradiction?"

Again I do not want to play coy. "Yes, it is, but life is filled with all sorts of paradoxes. I bet you feel like I am a man beyond redemption?"

"No man is beyond redemption; that's why I believe in the Gospel," Minister Blackwell replies.

Minister Blackwell's words inspire me. I sit beside the pulpit alongside Pastor Robinson and soak in all of the praises the saints give on to God. Praise and worship is in full swing, absent Kanisha, who had to work. Pastor Robinson once again stares into the deep abyss. Ever since I dropped the news that her husband might've been murdered or badly injured, Pastor Robinson seems to mentally check out.

I've stayed in contact with Spider and he's checked all of the hospitals and nothing has come up under Tony Robinson. At this point I am certain that Tony had skipped town under the nose of Spider. I would have to follow up with Spider later, but for now I have a sermon to preach and for the first time in a long time I am excited to minister the Word of God.

"Didn't our hearts burn with gladness from the Word? We were blessed the other night by Minister Dungy and he's back to bless us again with the Word. Jubilee Temple, please give him a warm welcome and tell him to preach!"

"Preach!" the church says in an ecstatic manner.

I plan to preach and I plan to preach in a manner that is worthy of my calling. I approach the pulpit with confidence and pride.

"Praise the Lord, saints. I said praise the Lord." I do not feel phony in my praise. The congregation receives me and Pastor Robinson looks on, not amused. *I bet she wonders if this is all an act.*

"Matthew 26:31. 'Then Jesus said to them, you will all be offended and stumble and fall away because of me this night.'" Just as I did with the Bible Study, I decide to come off the pulpit and walk down to the front row. "We all know that this is the part of the Gospel where Peter talks real big about how he would follow Jesus until the end and Jesus predicts that he would deny Christ three times."

I receive a few amens, but not a lot. I am sure this does not sound like a "Double for Your Trouble" sermon, but I have a point that I need to make. "Jesus already knew that Peter would fail this test, but how many of you know that God gives make-ups?"

More amens start to pour in and my adrenaline starts to kick in.

"How many of you know that God already knows that you're going to fall, but He made sure that you won't fail?" I raise my hand in agreement with my own statement.

Now I have the whole congregation behind me with full support. I even look back at Pastor Robinson and see a smirk on her face. "How many of you know that no one is outside of God's plan for redemption?"

A third of the congregation is on their feet, clapping and praising God.

"And just when you think you're beyond redemption, that's when Jesus shows up." The church explodes and I feel more alive at this moment than I have felt in years.

After the service I am greeted by Sister Victory Morgan, the greeter who I bumped into at the previous services.

"That was an awesome sermon," Victory says.

"Thank you very much, Sister Morgan. To God be the glory."

"Listen, I don't know how long you're in town for, but on Sunday my family and I get together for dinner and we would love to have you over."

"Oh, I don't know if that would be such a good idea."

"I tell you what. Have a little taste of my pot roast and then question whether you made the right decision."

I cannot put my finger on it, but Victory has something special within her. I can read people better than most prosecutors, but I do not know Victory's angle. All I know is that the last thing I need is a date.

"I'm sorry but I can't!" I say. Then again, I could be wrong. A date might be just what I need.

Chapter Eighteen

"He struck again," Spider says with the news playing. There is another murder not three days from the first murder. Police still have not identified the first victim.

"It gets worse." Spider places his tablet over an old pizza box and he has both a map and a pattern outlined in the shape of a triangle. "I observed the pattern. He's working this one controlled area; strangely, where he started was in the same area where people last saw your boy." Spider points to a spot on the map. Spider has all but concluded that Tony Robinson has been murdered by the Husband Stalker.

"But we don't know for sure if my guy was murdered?"

"No, but we do know that the last time anyone ever saw your boy was around this area before he disappeared." Spider has a sly grin on his face. He is intrigued by the fact that he can catch a modern-day psycho and I am dumbfounded by the fact that I might have to confess to the church that the first gentleman has been murdered.

There's a knock on the door and Spider springs to his feet. Spider opens the door and Paul is on the other side with a file under his arm, a pizza in one hand, and a six pack of beer in the other.

"What have I missed?"

"I figured out his patterns." Spider takes the pizza and beer and sets the pizza on top of the table after I moved the map.

Spider dives right into the pizza and files. After a brief prayer I grab a slice of pizza and sort through my own notes on the case.

"You want one?" Paul asks while holding up a beer. Paul is surprised that Spider doesn't want a beer, but he is even more surprised that I don't want a beer either.

"Seriously?" Paul asks.

"Yeah, man, I'm just trying to keep my head clear," I say.

"Okay, well, you're going to drive me back to the hotel." Paul takes a swig of his beer and a bite of his pizza.

We could be three college buddies kicking back, talking about the good old days; instead we are locked into a case that will dramatically impact our lives. For Spider it will be a healthy bounty for catching a serial killer, and for Paul it means his long-elusive Pulitzer. For me I don't know what it means. All I know is that I need to focus on the facts as they pertain to the case and not get caught up in the pursuit of a serial killer.

"Here's what we got so far. There's a homeless man who says he saw a tall figure in a hooded sweatshirt dump the rolled-up carpet in a Dumpster before getting into a gray truck," Paul says.

"That truck is probably gone by now. He's using different cars, which means we ought to look into any stolen cars lately."

"Way ahead of you. I took a look into reported stolen cars and none of them match the truck that was stolen."

"That means he either stole it a long time ago or he bought it a long time ago," I say.

Paul points at me as if I am right on the money. Paul and Spider continue their conversation, and while I am intrigued by the whole serial killer situation, I have to work off of the facts. I know that it has been almost three weeks now since Pastor Robinson has seen her husband.

It's been two weeks since any coworker has seen Tony and that is also the last time Sister Deborah has seen Tony as well. Spider checked family and all forms of transportation and it came up empty.

"What you got over there?" Paul asks.

I look up and see that Paul is very interested in what I am doing. "Nothing!"

"Don't ask me to share information and you're being stingy."

Of course the whole case has thrown me for a loop. *Maybe a fresh set of eyes would help me.*

"Listen, no matter what I say, this stays between us, you understand?"

I get head nods from both Spider and Paul. That will have to suffice.

"I was supposed to help this church find their pastor's husband who has gone missing, but now I think he might be a victim of the Husband Stalker."

"So you got a church that paying you to pay me twenty grand?" Spider asks.

"I got a church that's paying me $150,000."

Both Spider's and Paul's mouths drop. "Nic, you got to let me look into their financials," Paul says.

"No one is to know. My business is based on secrets and service. The second word gets out that I can't be trusted, and then I'm as good as dead."

"I'm not going to do a story, but at least let me get a look at their financials, because that might be the missing link to your case."

I have forgotten all about the mystery surrounding who is paying me. Paul is right and I should let him do what he does best and look into the financial records.

"Okay, but promise me that as soon as you find something, you'll call me."

"You got my word!" Paul says.

It feels good to have someone to trust in this game. I will need someone to trust before this is all over and right now Paul and Spider are the only two who I can trust.

Chapter Nineteen

It is Sunday and this marks almost two weeks since I first touched down in Sacramento. I am not any closer to finding Tony Robinson. His trail has turned cold and I fear for the worst. The only thing that I have gotten closer to is God. It is nice for a change to embrace a spiritual connection with my Lord and Savior that for so long has remained dormant.

Pastor Robinson and Minister Blackwell manage to convince me to preach the eleven o'clock service. Minster Blackwell says that the congregation is excited about my arrival and that has caused enough of a distraction to keep the talks about the first gentleman's absence to a minimum. However, this is more than a diversion for me; I can't put into words what I feel. At best I can describe my feeling as something sweet like nectar. My spirit is high and like the Prophet Nehemiah, I don't want to come down.

I approach the pulpit as I have done before, but this time there is no connection with my sermon. I plan to preach from the famous passage in Hebrews that Christians have dubbed the Hall of Fame passage. It is a passage that speaks of the heroes of faith and it is designed to inspire people to also become their own hero in faith. But that is not what God is telling me in my spirit. No matter how I try to review my notes, I feel my spirit tell me to pray. The request started off subtle, but now it has a firm lock on me to pray, and who am I to argue with the Holy Spirit?

"I had a sermon prepared, but I have to be obedient to the Holy Spirit and the Holy Spirit is leading me to pray." I step down from the pulpit and stand in the front pew. "There's someone here who desperately needs prayer and with all of the saints praying I know that we can get both an answer and a breakthrough today. So come down to the altar right now for prayer."

After a moment of awkwardness, a woman makes her way down the aisle. The navy blue business suit complements her pale yellow skin. I admire the woman's courage; no one wants to be the first unless there is something that the individual really needs. Minister Blackwell comes down and takes the microphone from me because no one else needs to know what we are praying about.

"What's going on, sister?" I say in her ear.

"I went to the doctor the other day and they found some black spots on my liver. I need prayer."

I start to pray for this beautiful, strong woman and I lose control of my words and speech. I place my hands on her head and I feel her body sway. I hear her speaking in tongues and crying out to the Lord and I open my eyes and she has left. Another woman approaches. The girl couldn't be a day over nineteen. The girl has on a white tank top with a pair of jeans that are ripped in the front. To be blunt, I've met prostitutes who conceal more.

"What's going on, sister?" I say.

"I need prayer. I'm trying to get out of this abusive relationship before this girl kills me." I went right into the prayer and I can hear her, like the woman before, cry and sob. I feel like the spirit of heaviness is being lifted from not only the girl, but from me as well. When I open my eyes this time, there is a line that wraps around the sanctuary. The Holy Spirit moves throughout Jubilee

Temple and while physically I am exhausted spiritually I never felt stronger. One by one each individual comes up for prayer, and one by one they leave fulfilled. I have seen and experienced a lot of things in my walk with God; today's service is undoubtedly a first.

After service, some of the saints remain and continue to praise God and shout. I myself am still on a spiritual high, but I need Pastor Robinson to meet with me in her office. This case has not played out like how I would've expected it to play out. I am in the back of the office with Pastor Robinson doing some work. Pastor Robinson's attention is locked in to what is going on in the sanctuary. Every whoop and holler causes her to peek her head up to see. *What is going on?* For a second I think she has X-ray vision and can see through the walls of her office. Today's service can't even be put into words. Even with the service being over for at least a half an hour now, there are still people in the sanctuary being delivered from whatever yoke that was tied around their necks and the church still feels vibrant.

I hate my ability to read people because it takes away the freedom to be naïve, the freedom to take someone at their word. I called the meeting to see if there is any other information Pastor Robinson could lend to help me find her husband. I abandoned the wild goose chase that her husband has been savagely murdered. The whole idea of her husband being murdered leaves something to be desired. I have to focus on reality and reality is that Tony Robinson has disappeared and he needs to be found.

"So when did you change?" Pastor Robinson asks.

"Change what?"

Pastor Robinson sits back in her chair with a smile that can only be interpreted as sarcastic. "Obviously judging by today you have the anointing. You must've stood in my position at one point in time and you're a long ways from being the minister you originally set out to be. So what changed?"

"How much time do you have?" I reply.

We both share a laugh and that is a rare moment for the two of us.

"I was helping this one church out of Memphis. Some of the prominent members of the church were real suspicious about the pastor and how the church funds were being spent. So I went and, my goodness, this man could speak." I shake my head as I reflect. "He could talk you right out of your wallet. I checked the church financial records and nothing. He was squeaky clean. So I had a private investigator who was a friend of mine check his personal financial records and sure enough it turns out that the pastor was a scam artist and that he had ripped off more than half of his members." I shrug my shoulder as if there was no need to go further.

"How?" Pastor Robinson asks.

"The pastor would travel to different places and preach about stepping out on faith. He would ask ten people to step out on faith and when they did, he would reward them a hundred dollar bill. The church would run and shout and act up." I do a gesture with my hands to try to liven up the mood but to no avail. Pastor Robinson is not amused. "Anyway he would ask the same people he gave a hundred dollars to step out on faith and give him back ten dollars. Tithe!"

"And would they do it?" Pastor Robinson asks.

"Yes, they would, but most of the members didn't have ten dollars on them, so they would write a check. The pastor would then take the check and give it to his crew and they would hack into the member's account and drain it."

My story finally sparks a dropped jaw from Pastor Robinson. "How come they didn't know?"

"Because the pastor's crew had set up so many firewalls and dummy accounts and businesses that the information was never recovered. But this is the most disturbing part: because no one wanted to believe that a man of God was capable of doing something like that."

"So why continue to work in ministry?"

I don't know how to answer that question. What am I to say? Because I get paid handsomely or because part of me still believes that I can change the world? "I'm too old to go and play for the Lakers."

Pastor Robinson gives me another smirk and it is good to see her attempt to smile. "So what do you need from me?"

"We went through the normal channels and could not find your husband."

"I thought you would've found him by now!" Pastor Robinson stops reading her Bible.

"So did I, which is why I think something might've happened to him."

Pastor Robinson's whole countenance changes. My only criticism of Pastor Robinson is her lack of emotions. Pastor Robinson shows true concern for her husband. "Are you telling me that you think my husband might've been butchered?"

"Listen, I understand your concern for your husband. We're going to find him." I pivot around the desk and kneel down before Pastor Robinson, who is sobbing in her seat.

"Listen, I need you to think really hard. Your husband must've gone back to his roots or something. Was there any relationship prior to you?"

"Before me, my husband was not the relationship type. He had a series of flavors of the month before he finally settled down with me."

I know that Pastor Robinson is sincere in what she says, but I also know that she is sincerely wrong. No man goes from being a playboy to settling down and getting married without there being at least one woman who introduces the idea that even a playboy can settle down.

"You know that there is a serial killer on the loose," Pastor Robinson says.

I am surprised that Pastor Robinson is able to tear herself away from her Bible long enough to be aware of anything current.

"Don't worry about it. Your husband is okay," I say as I stand up and head toward the door. "I'm going to go check on what's going on outside."

I exit the office and I make my way down the hall. I stand just outside of the sanctuary and observe the people in the sanctuary who are still praying. It is a nice day, which is a nice change for November, when things have been very gloomy.

Victory caught my peripheral vision with both her smile and her form-fitting white-blazer-with-gold-trim business suit. "Do you always have to look so serious?"

"That's my signature look."

"So where does the mighty Minister Dungy eat? I hope you don't take me as being forward."

I remember Victory's offer earlier in the week to come over to her house for dinner. I wonder if it is too late to accept the invitation.

"I prefer forward, and to answer your question, I usually have my food served to me through a drive-thru window."

"Aw, that's sinful. Well like I said before, my family and I get together after church every Sunday for dinner. You are invited."

"Thanks, but I don't play well with others."

"That's fine, because my family and I don't play fair."

I laugh and enjoy Victory's sharp wit. She has a glow that I find appealing.

"Okay, well, is there anything that you want me to bring?"

She flashes me a smile that conveys more than what she says. "No, we're good; we break bread at six P.M."

"See you then."

I arrive at Victory's address. She lives in a traditional suburban two-story home in the corner of a cul-de-sac. I ring the doorbell and moments later Victory opens the door with an apron on.

"God bless you, Minister Dungy," Victory says with a smile.

"Good evening, and God bless, and I hope that this isn't interpreted as being forward or inappropriate." I reveal a bottle of wine.

"Not at all. I enjoy a good glass of Moscato every now and again." Victory takes the bottle of wine and opens the door wide enough for me to enter.

I enter the home and hear salsa music. "Don't mind us. We like to have fun. Let me introduce you to my family."

Victory takes me around her house and introduces me to her two brothers, and her Auntie Rose. I even meet Victory's parents by way of a huge portrait that hangs above the fireplace. Both of Victory's parents died within five years of each other. Her father, Jim Morgan, died from congestive heart failure and her mother, Tiffany Morgan, died of a broken heart, Victory says.

I see people salsa dancing as I follow Victory to the kitchen. A little five-feet-five-inches-tall spitfire of a girl stands in my way and prevents me from moving.

"You have to dance with me first."

My mother used to teach dance and I have not forgotten all that she taught. I start to salsa with the girl. This is a vibrant group of people. I expect to hear Mahalia Jackson and see a ten-pound Bible. I salsa my way into the kitchen and leave the girl spinning.

"Nice. A minister who can dance, preach, and pick a good Moscato," Victory says.

"I became all things to all men so that I might win some."

Victory is in the process of mashing up potatoes. I can smell the garlic. "I've never seen anything like that today. What God did through you was amazing."

"Yes, it was, which is good because I'm not really a Sunday kind of preacher."

"Well, I enjoy your sermons. So where are you from, Minister Dungy? It's like you appeared out of nowhere like a ghost."

And like a ghost I shall leave. There is no room in my world for a relationship or marriage. "I stay on the road so much that I don't really have a home."

"And how does that sit with Mrs. Dungy?"

I chuckle because she couldn't be any more blatant, but she has charm.

"I wouldn't dare put a woman through my schedule. I already have a hard enough time keeping up with my schedule."

I can tell that Victory is disappointed by my statement, but I would rather she be disappointed than heartbroken.

"A man should have a good home to go to. It's not good for a man to be alone."

"I find satisfaction in how many men I get back to their homes."

All of a sudden a Nerf ball hits Victory on the shoulder, followed by a procession of laughter. Victory puts down the mashed potatoes and grabs the ball.

"And you wonder why you didn't play Division I baseball." Victory throws the Nerf ball and hits a man squared in the head. There is another procession of laughter.

"Pretty good," the guy says as he picks up the Nerf ball.

Victory resumes her duties of preparing the meal. "I'm sorry. My brother is . . . stupid!"

"No apologies necessary. You played sports?" I ask.

"Softball in high school and college. I played at Arizona State."

Victory finishes with her preparation and starts to set the tables.

"I'm ready!" Victory yells and we all assemble around the table.

There is a nice spread of food from the pot roast to the garlic mashed potatoes and a green salad. We all take each other's hands.

"Go ahead, Minister Dungy," Victory says.

I feel Victory nudge my hand and I know that I can't pass the buck. "Everyone with bowed heads."

We pray and it is the first time I've prayed in public over a meal in a long time. What is going on inside of me is both strange and great. It is great because I can feel myself change for the better, but it is strange because I feel like I am changing to the person I used to be. For the first time in God knows how long, I sit at a table and have a good meal and decent conversation, with Victory and the members of her family.

"So, Minister Dungy, what did you think about the pastor who killed himself about a month ago?" Mark, Victory's brother, asks.

I almost choke on my food. I'd prefer for the conversation to remain on whether the 49ers were Super Bowl contenders and if Obama would get a second term. Anything but a conversation about Pastor Lewis.

"I think it was a sad state of affairs," I say.

"Did you know him?" Mark asks.

"I had met him a few times and I thought I knew him, but I was wrong."

"I wonder what would cause a pastor of all people to commit suicide," Aunt Bay says before she takes a sip of her wine.

The answer is the guy at your table. The guy who brought you the wine is responsible for the minister's death. "We can't judge people because only God know what's in their heart."

"All I know is that . . . that was real sad," Victory says.

"But there is something to be said about a man of God, a minister, who resorts to such a cowardly act," Tiffany, Victory's sister, says.

"Not a coward," I say, unsure if I want anyone to hear it.

"What else would he be if not a coward?" Tiffany replies.

"I don't know . . . a hopeless individual, but not a coward. It's not easy to end one's life; otherwise, none of us would be sitting here, because we have all found ourselves at a low point. And yet we keep on because we are products of hope. For someone to come to a point where hope is not enough is a lot of things, but I wouldn't be quick to call him a coward," I say.

"Well said, Preacher," Mark replies.

"I don't know. I just think that an ambassador of faith and hope should be able to walk out their faith," Tiffany says.

"I agree with you, but in the real world we see our leaders fall flat on their faces all the time. None of us make it through life unscathed, so I wouldn't be quick to call someone a coward or otherwise if they can't see beyond the moment."

"Well, you just put me in my place, Mr. Preacher," Tiffany replies with a roll of the neck.

"It happens," I say and the rest of the table bursts into laughter.

Thank God for the laughter because it turns the conversation to other, trivial things. Pastor Lewis reminds me of my failure as a problem solver and, for his sake and mine, I can't afford to fail Pastor Robinson.

Chapter Twenty

The next day I get a call from Paul and he asks me to meet him at the Golden Corral restaurant. I do not know what made Paul want to meet with me at Golden Corral, but I know it must be important so I decide to go and meet my friend at the restaurant. I pull up next to Paul's rental car. Paul rented a maroon Chrysler after I picked him up from the airport and dropped him off at his hotel. I get out of my car and I get into the passenger side of Paul's car. Paul's body language conveys that he has no intention of going inside of the restaurant.

"I guess you got a hankering for yeast rolls," I say to Paul in an attempt to lighten the mood. All Paul gives me is pursed lips and an awkward stare, as if I am in trouble. "What?"

"Do you know how much I love you?" Paul asks but he does not allow me to respond. "I love you so much that I can't stand you right now."

"Boy, if you don't start making sense . . ."

"And if you don't start telling me what's going on with you and this church, then I'm going to run this story in the paper tomorrow."

My heart sinks. My whole business and credibility will be compromised if word gets out about this case. "I'm here helping a pastor find her husband."

"Are you sure about that? Is that your story that you're sticking to?"

Anger rises up in me. I no longer see Paul as my friend but a scumbag of a reporter.

"Hold on now. You gave me your word. Now you offered to look into the source of the money. You promised that if I let you look into the financial records you wouldn't run the story. Your word may not mean much to you, but it means something to me."

Paul lets out a sinister grin and then he lets out a demented laugh. It takes a lot of self-control for me not to punch him in the face. I hate someone knowing something I don't know and I hate someone gloating even more.

"Luckily I don't have many friends so I see no need in losing any." Paul picks up the file and hands it to me. "I found out who's paying you. Your fee may have come from the church but the money came from another source."

What else is new? That is one thing I can say about Paul; he has a flair for the dramatic. I open the file and on the first page is a copy of my check and on the next page is a copy of a deposit made by Another Level Productions. "What's Another Level Productions?"

"I have to remind myself how green you are at times. Another Level Productions is one of the biggest adult film industries on the West Coast. They film movies out in San Fernando Valley but the office of the CEO, Brian Perkins, is based out of San Francisco."

Now that is a surprise, that my fee is being paid by a CEO in the porn industry. Why would the church have any ties to the porn industry? Unless there is someone who is affiliated with the adult film industry. "Thank you, Paul. This information has really helped me out."

"You owe me," Paul says.

"Put it on my tab," I reply. "So do you want to go in here and grab lunch?"

"I just finished eating. I got to run. I'll see you later and let me know how that lead turns out," Paul says.

"Will do." I get out of the car and go inside. I figure I can get a good meal while I thumb through the file.

The restaurant has a pretty good crowd for a Monday afternoon. Now, as a kid I was fond of old movies that starred Clark Gable and Paul Newman. Those guys were so cool and I think my infatuation with smoking stemmed from those legendary actors. But when I scan the restaurant, I feel more like Humphrey Bogart: out of all the restaurants in Sacramento, Victory has to be at the one that I decide to dine in.

Victory is by the salad bar and she is alone and her conservative white blouse and black skirt convey that she is on lunch break.

"Sir, are you going to eat?" the elderly cashier asks.

The cashier not only gets my attention, but she gets Victory's attention as well.

"Yes, I'm going to eat." I fumble through my pockets in search of money. I pay the cashier and Victory waits for me at the entrance of the different food stations.

"Stalker," Victory says.

"Yes, I know. I'm going to have to get a restraining order on you."

"Whatever! I see that you're alone. Want to be my lunch date?" Victory asks.

"Sure." Before I can say anything else, Victory takes me by the arm to the salad bar and leads me through the various stations.

"Don't forget to try the yeast rolls," Victory says.

I grab two yeast rolls just to appease her. We grab a booth at the corner of the restaurant and share laughs between bites.

"I can't believe you survived a whole dinner with my family."

"Your family is not that bad. Trust me. I've seen worse."

Victory smiles and for a few minutes she looks as if she is going to say something, but instead she stuffs her mouth with her salad.

"I really like hanging out with you," I say.

"Me too. This is nice, this is fun. We should do this more."

"I wish we could, but in truth I'm not that guy."

"What guy?" Victory asks.

"The type of guy who could do this." I gesture with my hands. "That's not me. I've always been terrible with relationships."

"Who's to say I want a relationship?" Victory said.

Victory's statement chips away at my ego. "Well, what is this to you? What do you want it to be?"

"What it is—uncomplicated." She smiles.

She is preaching to the choir with that statement. "Look, Victory, you're like this huge magnet and I can't shake the fact that I'm drawn to you. I just don't want you to be disappointed."

"I'm a big girl. I can handle disappointments."

I wish I could shed this mentality and develop a more positive one where couples get married for the right reasons and stay married for the right reasons as well. If I could adopt that kind of mentality then and only then could I entertain a future with Victory. But now is the essence of my domain and now is not the time to consider love and happiness.

"Can I ask you something?" Victory asks.

"You strike me as a woman who doesn't need permission to ask anything. Go ahead." I gesture for Victory to go on.

"Why here? Why Jubilee Temple?"

"What do you mean?"

"You're a traveling evangelist, I assume, and of all of the churches you pick ours to help out. Sure, we're not a store front church but we're not a mega church neither, so why here?"

"Let's just say I was called."

"You must have a powerful anointing," Victory says.

I haven't thought about my anointing until the other day when I prayed for the congregation. Prayer is such a vital tool in the Christian walk, and when I went full-fledged into ministry, I was a prayer warrior. Until recently I prayed over my food, while driving, and little micro prayers throughout the day, but nothing like the other day. God is in the process of awakening something that has lain dormant in my spirit. Maybe after this job, I can begin to seek a life beyond the problem-solving business.

"Before I leave, I want to take you out on a real date," I say.

"And I just might be inclined to go." We both share a laugh and a meal.

Chapter Twenty-one

Another Level Productions has an office in downtown San Francisco inside a five-story post-modern building. I don't know what to expect as I enter the building. I guess I am expecting half-naked women to be walking around and followed by adoring fans and cameramen. That is not the case. At first glance this doesn't seem like a place where a top adult film executive would have their office. This seems like a building for lawyers or accountants, but then again the best place to hide is in plain sight. I weave my way through heavy foot traffic and approach one of the security guards at the desk.

"Nicodemus Dungy to see Brian Perkins." I hand the security guard my ID.

The security guard takes my ID and checks it with his current information. He then hands me a visitor's pass and I go on with my job. "Thank you."

I enter a busy elevator lobby and watch as the numbers on the elevator count down to the lobby floor. When the elevator arrives I enter along with several other business execs. I am heading to the third floor, which means I have a short but uncomfortable ride ahead of me.

When I arrive at the third floor I am amazed at how quiet the floor is compared to some of the other floors that I get a glimpse of while on the elevator.

"How may I help you?" a pretty secretary asks.

"Nicodemus Dungy to see Brian Perkins."

"His office is to your left."

I walked down a long, narrow hallway to Brian Perkins's office. I knock on the door.

"It's open!" I hear from the other side of the door.

I open the door and there is Brian Perkins both on the office phone and texting.

"Look, man, there's a lot of money riding on this. You need to talk to your girl and get her on board." Brian makes eye contact with me. "Hey, let me hit you back later." Brian Perkins hangs up the phone and sizes me up and I have already sized him up. He's a short guy.

"Hi, Nicodemus Dungy."

"Brian Perkins." He shakes my hands. "Have a seat."

I observe the pictures on the walls of provocative women and adult movie titles. The pictures hang on Brian's wall like gold records.

"I bet you got some stories to tell me because Christians are the biggest freaks."

"I don't know what you're talking about," I reply.

"You don't know what I'm talking about? You're walking around with my money in your pocket. What do you mean you don't know?"

This guy knows a whole lot about my profession and I don't like that. All the information I have on him came from the Internet.

"When Li-Li called me and told me that she needed a huge favor. I knew that it had to be big."

"Li-Li?"

"Oh, you don't know. Oh, this is too good." Perkins starts to dance up and down in excitement. "This is too good."

Brian hops up and goes over to his flat-screen TV where he has a DVD player play a movie that is already in the DVD player. Moments later I see an intense sex scene already in progress.

"Anyone look familiar?" Brian says.

Brian has such a smug disposition, but when I look closer I do see someone who looks familiar. On closer observation I see a younger and thinner Pastor Latonya Robinson. The image will forever be burned into my memory. I suspected that Pastor Robinson was not being upfront with me, but never in a million years did I expect to see a movie with her engaging in the horizontal polka.

"Okay, that's enough." I motion for Brian to turn the movie off.

"Yeah, she was one of my best. Man, she was talented. Sexy, smart, and, boy, she made me a lot of money." Brian shakes his head.

Brian goes on to talk about Pastor Robinson as if she were a poet or a musician. All I saw was a misguided girl who now did everything in her power to erase the past.

"So what happened?" I ask.

"Before her dude disappeared, I didn't know. She just up and left. Gone! Cut off all contact. Then one day I get a call from her and she tells me that she's a minister and that she needs to hire some guy to find him."

"So you gave her a loan?" I ask.

"Oh no, sir!" Brian sits up in his chair. "I'm not a bank. I don't give loans. That's her money. At the time when Li-Li left she had just finished four movies and I was waiting for the money to come in. She knew that and she never needed that money until now. You can say what you want about me, but I ain't no crook."

Good thing I am sitting down because my head is spinning. I need to have a talk with Pastor Robinson, aka "Li-Li."

Chapter Twenty-two

"Come on, Nic! Pull yourself together!" I have to tell myself because this is the second time I almost rear-ended someone since I left the Another Level Productions office. My body is physically in the car but my mind is divided between Tony Robinson and his wife's freaky past. Though I know where I am heading next, I have no sense of direction in regard to this case. I travel along the 580 toward Stockton where I am sure to find Pastor Robinson.

The meeting at Brian Perkins's office was surreal. At the same time the revelation that Pastor Robinson used to be a porn star starts to come into focus. I now understand why Pastor Robinson has such a strong ministry with women and such a lousy marriage. Pastor Robinson specializes in women who have been written off by society. I can only imagine how long Tony Robinson knew about his wife's past before he decided to leave. I began this journey with a lot of unanswered questions; now I have only a few questions and only one person who can answer them.

"Sisters, we have to become virtuous women. Women who personify the scriptures," Pastor Robinson says.

As agreed, Pastor Robinson has turned over most of her services to her ministerial staff. Pastor Robinson does, however, keep her speaking engagements. I am in attendance at the Virtuous Women conference in Stockton and I watch on as Pastor Robinson speaks.

"We all know that Ruth was a virtuous woman but as the scriptures say, we are living epistles and each of us has an epistle to write. Your story doesn't end with drug abuse; your story doesn't end with prostitution; your story doesn't end in welfare. No, virtuous women of God, your story is written by the master and he says in Jeremiah 29:11 that God plans to give hope and an expected end. You story ends with praise. " Pastor Robinson looks up and makes eye contact with me and she is thrown off. Women started to turn their heads to get a peek at the shadowy figure in the back that threw Pastor Robinson off her game.

After the workshop I weave through a crowd of women chitchatting and I find Pastor Robinson engaged in an intense conversation with a small group of women. Pastor Robinson is never lacking in passion, I'll give her that. She shows conviction in everything that she does. When she makes eye contact with me a second time she dismisses the group and I wait until there is no one within earshot to talk.

"Please tell me you have good news."

"Not really. I had a meeting with your old buddy Brian Perkins."

If Pastor Robinson could, she would have turned white. Instead her eyes enlarge and Pastor Robinson puts her hands on her throat as if she is choking.

"We need to talk," I say.

"Not here." That's all Pastor Robinson says before she starts walking and heads up the aisle toward the exit. I follow Pastor Robinson up the aisle and out of the sanctuary.

We do not stop in the lobby, but make a hard left to a narrow hallway with office doors on each side. Pastor

Robinson stops at the office before the last office on the left-hand side and enters. I follow Pastor Robinson and close the door behind us.

"Correct me if I'm wrong, but you were supposed to be looking for my husband and not prying into my personal life," Pastor Robinson says.

"Your personal life has relevance with your husband's disappearance. Especially when a guy finds out that his wife is a former adult film star."

The weight of her past causes Pastor Robinson to fall back into her seat. I know that she wishes her past would stay hidden, but we can't hide from our past. We have to expose it and let it go.

"So let me guess. Tony discovers you she hid a big secret from him and bounces."

"Our marriage had gone cold. We had not been on the same page in a long time. And throw in the fact that we hadn't had sex in months and you can see that a man will explore other options to get satisfaction."

"So one day he puts in a movie and, lo and behold, he sees his sanctified wife engaged in some hardcore porn," I say, and a tear falls down Pastor Robinson's face.

"I grew up in a strict home. I went to church every time the doors were open. I wasn't even allowed to watch PG-13 movies. I ran away from home at fifteen and you know the rest of the story."

I do. Unfortunately I do know the rest of the story. Pastor Robinson became desperate, and one cannot build a life out of desperation. I'm sure Pastor Robinson wouldn't be able to tell how she went from being a church girl to a porn star, but it happens and in her case it happened.

"So what happened?" I ask.

"One night I was on my way to a shoot and I got lost. I saw this middle-aged woman walking with a Bible in her hand, headed to this church. I stopped the woman

and told her that I was lost and she said, 'You sure are!'"
Pastor Robinson chuckles as she wipes the tears from her
eyes. "She convinced me to come with her to the church
and I got saved right then and there."

Pastor Robinson has a powerful testimony. Her journey from adult film star to a prominent pastor reminds
me of the power of the Gospel. The Gospel is the good
news that we all can be transformed and become what
God originally designed us to become. Despite the power
behind Pastor Robinson's testimony, I am a man of
principle and of rules; and rules have been broken.

"So what happens now?" Pastor Robinson asks.

"Now I leave. I go back home."

"Excuse me?" Pastor Robinson stands up.

"I live and operate by a strict code and one of my rules
is no lies. I'm not the guy you lie to. You pay me to both
keep and clean your dirty little secrets, and once you lie to
me then the trust is broken."

"You should understand why I wouldn't tell you."

"You should've told me the truth. You left out a criti-
cal piece of this case and had me spinning my wheels,
worried that your husband might've been murdered. It
never occurred to you to tell me that maybe the reason
why your husband disappeared was because he found out
about your past."

"Yes, he found out about my past. He found out that
the reason why his wife is a little overweight is because
I went through a deep depression after I got saved and
found comfort in food. He left because instead of having
the best sex of his life, he gets blank expressions and
halfhearted responses. What do you do when you've been
trained how to perform and nothing else?"

"I don't know. I don't know what to tell you." I don't
know what to tell Pastor Robinson. I don't know the first
thing about how hard her life was as a porn star, but I

didn't need to know to be helpful. I just needed her to trust me enough to help and she didn't.

"What about my husband?"

"I'm sorry but that's no longer my concern. I hope he does turn up." I turn away from Pastor Robinson and I head toward the door.

"You're a coward!"

I stop dead in my tracks, ready to go off. I don't turn around because I do not want to go off on Pastor Robinson because of the respect I have for her.

"I see why you couldn't hack it as a minister. You prefer covering up the muck instead of getting in there and actually making a difference."

"I never said I was a saint. I just know that I ain't a liar." Those are the last words I say before I leave the office.

Chapter Twenty-three

It has been almost a week since I have had a drink, but as I wait for my flight to board, I find myself at the bar with a tall glass of Heincken in front of me. I am beyond discouraged; not because Pastor Robinson has lied to me, but because the job is left unfinished. I have walked away from a job before and I didn't feel anything, but this is different. I have grown attached to the members of the church and I sincerely want to find Tony Robinson and talk with him. I guess the reason why I feel discouraged and guilty is because I knew that the reason why I walked away is a cop-out. I knew that Tony Robinson is long gone and rather than admit that, I used Pastor Robinson's past as a scapegoat.

"Breaking news. News of another murder in the Rancho Cordova area has citizens in the community alarmed," a reporter says.

"Turn it up!" I tell the bartender, who turns up the TV without hesitation.

I don't know why but reading the breaking news regarding another murder potentially done by the Husband Stalker makes me want to find him and bring him to justice. I am filled with an overwhelming sense to see this job to the end even if that means an end that I don't want to see. I get on the phone and call Spider.

"Hello?" Spider says.

"It's me! Come and get me! I'm at the airport."

"Good, because I got something," Spider says.

***

Back at Spider's house we try to figure out the Husband Stalker's next move. Spider has his tablet up with a map and all of the areas pinpointed where the police found the Husband Stalker's victims.

"This is what the police have found, but I did some digging and your reporter friend found out that the police did recover this." Spider pulls out a picture of a worn-out pair of pliers.

God only know what unspeakable horrors were committed with this tool. I imagine that the Husband Stalker took his time and inflicted as much suffering as he could on his victims before killing them.

"There's something special about these pliers. They aren't just any old pliers that you can get at Home Depot. These are pliers that are specifically sold at Ned's Depot," Spider says.

Ned's Depot is a chain of supply stores throughout the Bay Area. I am familiar with the store though I never really had a reason to go in there. Spider then brings up another map that has entirely different markings.

"These are the markings of the victims from the first time the Husband Stalker attacked." Spider points to a specific dot on his tablet. "This is where they found the first victim and this victim was found less than five miles from a Ned's Depot."

Spider then goes back to the original screen. "Here is where we found the first victim after the Husband Stalker resurfaced."

Spider points to another spot on the map and I can put two and two together. The first victim, who I pray was not Tony Robinson, was found not too far from a Ned's Depot location. That piece of information tells me two things: the killer is a creature of habit and that his patterns will be what leads to his downfall.

"Not too far from this Ned's location is a used car lot. According to this sales record, they most recently sold a gray truck to a Mulad Benson. I checked the name and the ID is a fake."

"Why would he buy a truck? Most serial killers would use a van or a car. Unless . . ."

"He needed to go off road!" Spider and I say in unison.

Spider saves his best for last when he shows pictures from what I can best describe as a bomb shelter. He even shows a spot where a piece of the wall has been carved and a small space that someone could sleep in has been made. It is a spot that only Spider could've found.

"We thought this whole time he was using the main road as an escape and really he was going underground."

"Is this . . . ?" I ask, and Spider gives me a head nod.

Spider then shows the previous screen from the first murders and the screen with this new pattern of murders. Both of them show the killer's trail going cold near a mountain range. I am so engulfed by the grim details of the Husband Stalker that I don't pay attention to the fact that Spider has left my side until I hear the sound of a shotgun being racked. I look up and see Spider with his twelve-gauge shotgun in hand.

"You feel like taking a ride with me?" Spider asks.

"I don't know . . . maybe!"

Chapter Twenty-four

Spider has a hunch and it means driving out to San Jose. I go along with Spider's theory because he is hardly wrong; and if we can put an end to this nightmare then so be it.

"So how do you know about this place?" I ask.

"Law enforcement and alcohol don't mix. Guys get together at a bar and start spilling secrets of bunkers hidden in the mountains in case of a doomsday scenario."

"So the Husband Stalker could be a cop?" I ask.

"Or an engineer, architect, or scientist. The spot we are going to has been abandoned; lack of funding, and I guess the government started to believe that the world wasn't going to end anytime soon."

And that's the reason why I don't trust my government. Just imagine that our leaders, who are elected to serve us, are secretly meeting and plotting ways to insure their own survival. Politicians have one agenda and that is self-preservation.

"Oh, by the way, word is they identified the first victim . . . It wasn't your boy Tony. It was a stay-at-home father whose wife was in constitutional law," Spider says.

For some reason I knew that the first victim wasn't Tony, but that doesn't bring me any more comfort because I still don't know where Tony is.

"We got to find him," I say, though I'm not sure Spider hears me.

We drive off the 101 freeway into a mountain range. We go deep into the mountain, to the point where I am concerned that we won't make it back in one piece. This will be a waste of a trip if there is nothing here, but we keep on driving until we come upon a row of boulders. To the untrained eye the scene looks like normal wilderness, but I am sensing that there is something to how these boulders are positioned; in particular a boulder at the end that dwarfs all the other boulders.

Spider turns off the ignition and gets out of the car. He walks along the path of the boulders and I get out and follow him without saying a word. Spider stops at the large boulder at the end and after careful examination he tries to push. I try to give him a hand but Spider successfully pushes the boulder on its side.

"There we go." Spider is referring to a hatch that is placed underneath the boulder.

I can't believe Spider is right; there is a bunker. It doesn't prove that the Husband Stalker hid here after he finished his string of murders, but it doesn't disprove it either.

"How many more of these bunkers are there?" I ask.

"Dozens throughout Northern California, but there's one in Sacramento that I'm curious about," Spider says.

I have done some stupid things in my life, but this by far wins the gold medal. We drive through the mountains on a hunch. A hunch that I pray to God Spider is wrong about; otherwise, we are about to encounter one of the most dangerous killers in the twenty-first century.

Darkness is all around and only a thin layer of light from Spider's truck shines. I thought this is a wild goose chase. I hoped that this is a wild goose chase, until Spider runs over something that makes an awkward noise on his truck.

"What was that?" I ask.

"I think it's what I'm looking for. Let go and see." Spider stops the car and I wish that I had not said anything.

Spider grabs his flashlight and exits the car. I get out and follow Spider. The wind chill is present and we walk only a few feet before we reach a metal plate. To say that it's awkward to come upon a metal plate in the middle of a mountain range is odd to say the least. Spider kneels down and uses his flashlight around the different corner. He sees a slight opening and he uses his index finger to try to pull up on the metal plate. The plate jerks back and Spider stands up.

"It's locked!" Spider starts to walk back to his truck.

I don't have to do too much speculation as to why there is a locked steel plate in the middle of the mountains. On the way Spider says that there were a few bomb shelters that were built as a precaution in case of a disaster. One of the many precautions our government officials took in a post-9/11 era. My heart is about to burst through my chest. Especially when I see Spider open up the back of his truck and get out his gear. He puts on a bulletproof vest, puts on his gloves, and then I grab his shotgun, a handgun and a Taser.

"Hold this." Spider hands me a set of bolt cutters. "You remember how to shoot?"

"Of course! " In college Spider used to take me to the gun range on several occasions.

"Let's hope you don't." Spider closes his truck then places the shotgun squarely on his shoulder.

We walk back to the steel plate and Spider rests the shotgun on the ground next to him and calls for the bolt cutters. The lock is positioned where someone could lock it from the inside; in fact, the lock itself is from the inside. I hand Spider the bolt cutters and after a few moments of maneuvering, Spider is able to clasp on to the lock and cut it open. He lifts the steel plate and looks down the hole with his flashlight. Sure enough, there is a set of stairs.

"I'll go first," Spider says, and there is no argument there.

Spider grabs his gun and goes down the set of stairs. I reluctantly follow and by the time I reach the bottom, Spider already has his shotgun up in firing position. I follow Spider at a safe distance. We walk through a hallway that is so narrow both of our shoulders brush up against the walls until we enter a space that is clean enough to perform surgery.

The room has a steel chair and to the right are a bunch of newspaper articles and clippings that sit above a computer. The image reminded me of a scene from the movie *Seven* when Morgan Freeman and Brad Pitt entered John Doe's apartment. The newspaper clippings tell a disturbing story of a deranged individual. To the left is a set of tools purchased from Serial-Killers-R-Us.

It happens too fast to recall, but I suddenly feel the presence of an individual up behind me. I turn around and all I see is a blur. All I can make out is an individual around my height with salt-and-pepper hair and beard. The image is superior in strength as the individual grabs a hold of my throat. I try to fight him off, but it seems useless. I try to go for the gun that Spider gave me, but I panic. All of a sudden I spin around and then I hear a loud thud and the individual loosens his grip on me until I am able to breathe again.

I fall on top of the individual who is now unconscious, and then roll over to the side as I try to catch my breath. Another image appears above me that is blurry until I make out that it is Spider.

"Thanks for keeping him distracted for me," Spider say.

I want to laugh, but at the moment I forget to laugh.

Chapter Twenty-five

I savor the smell of bacon. I thought that I might never get a chance to eat another piece of bacon, but as Spider, Paul, and I sit and eat breakfast, I give praise to the Lord.

"Thank you for the story, gentlemen. I'll make sure to include you in my Pulitzer speech."

Spider and I shake our heads.

"Let me know, what were you guys thinking?" Paul asks.

"I was thinking 'stop him before he takes another life,'" Spider says.

"I don't know if I was thinking at all," I say.

We eat breakfast and allow the sound of scraped forks and moaning be our conversation.

"So, Spider, I guess you got breakfast since you picked up a healthy bounty," Paul says in between sips of coffee.

Spider has collected a $200,000 bounty for the capture of the elusive Husband Stalker.

"I got breakfast, but to be honest with you. I'm probably going to donate most of the money to this youth center where I volunteer."

"I respect that!" Paul says.

"I do too and since you didn't find the guy I was looking for, I don't have to pay you the other half of your fee."

"Not so fast." Spider stops me and hands me an envelope. "I told you I would find him."

I open the envelope and sure enough, Spider is right.

***

Tamara Rhodes was a state champion in the long jump. Ms. Rhodes was also Tony Robinson's high school sweetheart. After high school they broke up because Tony wanted to focus on playing football. Tamara got married and changed her last name to Gibson. Tamara's husband, Todd Gibson, was killed in a car accident in 2007. The information that Spider left me showed that Tamara relocated from Richmond to Sacramento in 2010.

I stand outside of Tamara's townhouse and I ring the doorbell. Moments later a woman opens the door and I assume she is Tamara because her face is the same as the yearbook photo. She has the same shape and similar body shape as Pastor Robinson.

"Hi, can I help you?"

"Hi, my name is Minister Dungy and I was wondering if Tony Robinson was here?"

"What do you want?" an obviously male voice asks from the living room.

"I think you know what I want."

"It's okay," the man says.

Tamara steps aside and I enter the house and makes a beeline to the bedroom. On the couch is a man. When I finally get a good look at him I feel a wave of emotions. Tony Robinson sits on the couch watching *SportsCenter*.

"I've never seen you at the church before," Tony Robinson says calmly.

"I was asked to come in and intercede."

"There's nothing to intercede in. I'm done and I'm tired."

"I know what happened and I want to help."

"I don't think you do," Tony says.

"Oh, I do. I found out why you left and I understand. You have every right to be upset, but there are some people who are worried about you and need to know you're okay."

"You mean my wife? She finally notices me?" I look to Tamara, who is in the kitchen, fixing us something to drink. I looked back at Tony and he waves her off. "Don't worry about that. Tamara is an old friend and she was there when I needed her."

Tony has every reason to lie to me and yet I believe he is telling the truth about Tamara. Tony has remained faithful to his wife and I think that has a lot to do with his marriage vows and the fact that Tamara probably never got over the fact that Tony broke her heart.

"Listen, Tony. You're upset, I know. You've been betrayed, I know. If you want to walk then that's fine, but at least tell that to her face. You're a man's man; don't be a coward now. Face her and tell her what you want. Tell her how much she's betrayed you."

I know that I pushed it with the "coward" comment, but I can tell from Tony's body language that he is not easily offended. I just hope that he is willing to at least sit down and talk with his wife.

"I'm not a coward. When I found out, I wanted to grab my wife by the throat and squeeze and squeeze."

Tony did not grind his teeth when he spoke. He makes a strangling gesture with his hands as he speaks about his wife, but even that gesture is passive aggressive.

"She doesn't deserve him." Tamara sits down with a drink in hand. People lack civility, when I enter an apartment and not get offered a drink.

"Tammy, enough," Tony says.

"No! I'm not going to be quiet; not for you, or him." Tamara points at me. "Or for your wife. You deserve better. Do you know that he scored four touchdowns in the state championships?" Tamara says to me.

"Don't start that!" Tony says.

"It's the truth!" Tamara says. "I was head cheerleader. I was there."

"It's also the truth that we lost that game. My great game was overshadowed by a defeat. My whole life has been a series of humiliations and this one is the biggest one."

I lean forward and lock eyes with Tony. "Look, Tony, I know you feel like you've been kicked in the gut, but this is not the way a man resolves his issues. You don't have to sit on this couch with this lovely young lady and relive a time that's long gone."

"Who do you think you are coming up in my house like you the police?" Tamara stops talking when I hold up my finger.

"You've said enough." I look at Tony while I speak to Tamara. "Tony, at the very least talk with your wife before you consider leaving."

Tony does not respond to my request in words. The drop of his head tells me all I need to know.

Chapter Twenty-six

A suite at the Marriott in downtown San Francisco is not at all cheap, but the experience is minimal compared to the success that this meeting can produce. I enter the lobby of the hotel room and pick up my key. I carry a heavy duffle bag and make my way up to my room.

I step off the elevator and nervousness sets in my stomach. This is the first time I have done anything like this before. I will find out if this is something that I can get used to as far as couples counseling goes. I arrive at room 507 and slide the key card into the door. The light from the window illuminates the room, but I need a darker atmosphere. I set my bag down and cross the room over to the blinds. I close the blinds and a glimmer of light protrudes through the curtains.

I go back to my duffle bag and retrieve the contents of the bag: two small boxes filled with scented candles. I position the candles in different sections of the room. I made sure to get the candles with the short stems so that I don't start a fire. After the candles are lit I proceed to unpack expensive wine glasses, rose petals, massage oils, and all the other stuff I picked up based on suggestions from a cheesy magazine.

Twenty minutes later, I have ordered the food, and two bottles of wines are chilling in an ice bucket. There's a knock on the door and I sprint to the front door. I open the door and there is Tony Robinson on the other side.

"Come on in," I say as I open the door wide enough for Tony to walk in.

Tony Robinson enters the suite and takes a moment to observe the décor.

"I don't know about this, man," Tony says.

"Listen I'm the last person to advise you on what to do with your marriage. But I do know this; if you could just let her see you and just talk to her and hear you out, you'll feel a lot better about your decision."

All Tony can do is shake his head in agreement. His ego has been bruised, but there comes a point when a man has to stop running and take a stand. That's what this case has taught me: that I have to stop running from God because it is pointless. God is with me wherever I go.

I texted Pastor Robinson to meet me at the Marriott and that it was urgent. I didn't know how Pastor Robinson would respond to a text from a man to meet her at a hotel, but sure enough there is Pastor Robinson at the door.

"What is it, Minister Dungy? I thought you quit," Pastor Robinson says without any emotion.

I open the door and allow Pastor Robinson to see her husband at a candlelit dinner table.

"Oh my God." Pastor Robinson starts to shake, and the last thing I need is for Pastor Robinson to pass out. I take her by the hand and lead her into the hotel room.

The door closes and Tony Robinson gets up and walks over to Pastor Robinson. When Tony gets within a foot of Pastor Robinson, she slaps him and them she hugs him as if he is a ghost that had been resurrected back to life.

"I came to say good-bye," Tony says.

"I understand why you would want to leave and you have every right, but I prayed that God would give me a chance to tell you that I'm so sorry."

As I watch Pastor Robinson it is like she held all of her emotions back until this moment.

"Sorry doesn't begin to cover it," Tony says.

"I know. I just didn't want to lose you. You're a good man and I didn't want my past to ruin us."

"That pulpit ruined us a long time ago," Tony says.

"No, it didn't!" I reply.

"No disrespect, Nic, but you don't know," Tony says.

"I do know. If Pastor Robinson lied to you about her past then that means that there was a communication problem from the gate. You have to be completely honest with each other if your marriage is to even survive. The past and the pulpit are a direct result of your lapse of communication," I say.

"I'm sorry if I made you feel like you're second place in my life. I just wanted to be something other than an ex-porn star. I didn't want judgment; I just wanted to be free from my past."

"You could've told me," Tony says.

"You couldn't handle it," Pastor Robinson shot back.

"Would you want to be married to a man who couldn't handle your darkest secrets?" Tony shakes his head as if he already knows the answer.

"No," Pastor Robinson says, unable to make eye contact.

It is like I am not in the room, and I know that so long as Pastor Robinson and her husband are being honest, they might have a chance.

"So you found God and walked away from doing porn. Then you became a plain Jane in the bedroom."

"Please, I ain't no plain Jane. You wouldn't be able to handle the real me."

My mind flashes back to the young, misguided girl I saw in the video; that girl has become a grown woman. However, the grown woman has become insecure when it comes to matters of intimacy.

"Isn't that what marriage is suppose to be about? The real you?"

"It's hard for me to trust a man and be intimate with one. Every man in my life has exploited my sexuality and then I realized that I allowed them to. I don't know the first thing about how to be intimate and not trashy."

"It's about being able to take an unflinching look at each other, like what you're doing now," I say as I reach into my pocket and pull out a pack of nicotine gum. I am trying to quit, but as the saying goes, old habits die hard. I throw a couple of pieces in my mouth and savor the flavor before I continue. "What you guys are doing now should've been done a long time ago. More important than what the congregation, coworkers, or the world says about you is what God says about you and what you say about each other."

Neither Robinson responds to my statement. They just stare at each other like two sad star-crossed lovers. The room is less tense, but melancholy nonetheless.

"Knowing what you know now, could you even love me?" Pastor Robinson says with tears in her eyes.

"I never stopped. Despite how much it hurts and how embarrassed I felt, I loved you before I even knew you and that hadn't changed."

Pastor Robinson collapses in her husband's arms and she wails in joy. I think about what Minister Blackwell said to me recently. No one is beyond redemption.

"I'm going to let you guys have some privacy. I ordered a nice dinner on me that should be up in a little while, but before I do I just wanted to say this: fight for each other. If there was love there then it will remain," I say as I head out the door.

"Minister Dungy," Pastor Robinson says.

I turn around to look at her.

"Take care of yourself," Pastor Robinson says.

I give her a wink as I head out the door. I don't know if the Robinsons will reconcile. I just know that my work here is done.

Chapter Twenty-seven

The job is done, but I need to see Victory before I leave. This case was a mixed bag for me; on one hand I went to some dark places in order to uncover the truth. On the other hand this is the closest to normal I have ever felt, and this is the closest to God I have been in a long time. I need for this trip to end on a positive note and I can't think of a better place than along the boardwalk in Santa Cruz.

It takes Victory and me a couple hours to arrive at the beach. A week before Thanksgiving means that the weather is overcast, but none of that matters.

"You're too cool for me," Victory says before she takes a bite into her corn dog.

"Why you say that?"

"Look at you." Victory stops and examines me. "You're walking with your hands behind your back like you're a prince. Yeah, you're too cool for me."

"What can I say? I got tremendous swagger."

Victory and I share a laugh, then we share a sunset. We walk from the boardwalk onto the sand and sit down near the shore. Victory still has not finished her corn dog. We watch surfers skate along the water.

"Amazing, isn't it?" Victory points to the surfers.

"I know it take guts to get out there on those waves."

"One day I'm going to come into some money and then I'm going to spend the rest of my life surfing." Victory says.

"Sounds pretty ambitious." I pick up a handful of sand and let it slip through my fingers as I used to do when I was a kid.

"You care to join me?"

"I'll get back to you on that." My words are met with a playful shove by Victory. This moment is both real and special to the point where I don't want to waste it on fantasies of two lovers who forgot the world and live in pure bliss.

"You're no fun," Victory says.

"Of course I'm no fun, I'm a realist."

"It's realistic to be happy."

"Are you saying I'm not happy?" I ask.

"Not as happy as you could be."

Victory has a point. I am happy with her, but that happiness is dangerous, and I can't risk drawing Victory into my twisted world. Love is the ultimate risk and every day I see fools blindly risk everything for what they believe to be love.

"To be that happy would require for me to be a different person."

"Love just requires for you to be who you are and for someone to love you just as is. Isn't that what God teaches us?"

I answer Victory's question with a kiss. She doesn't pull away; instead Victory holds my lips firmly with hers and for a moment I am a guy who kisses a girl, nothing more. Victory pulls away and shows all of her whites.

I could've beheld her face all day, but I get a voice message from Minister Blackwell and I have to answer it.

"Hello?" I say.

"Get here now!" Minister Blackwell says.

"What is it?" Victory asks.

"We've got to go," I say and, like that, the moment is over.

***

I drive over to the church with Victory in the passenger seat of her own car. I drive unaware of the speed limits and unaware of the silent argument that Victory and I are having. This is not how I want the day to end. Victory is disappointed and her silence eats away at my conscience. This is why I can't get involved with someone. The church will always have a problem and will be in need of a problem solver.

Victory smiles and to the untrained eye, a smile is just a smile. Victory's smile is more cryptic.

"What?" I ask.

"Nothing. It's just that two hours ago you were smiling; then the church calls and now you're not."

"I was really enjoying the day with you." I can't even look at Victory. I feel bad enough.

"I was too, but ministry calls. I just wonder why doing the Lord's work causes you to become so stressed out."

"I guess it's an occupational hazard," I reply.

"It shouldn't be if you're spreading the good news."

I ponder Victory's observation for a moment, and then I disregard her statements altogether. Since the suicide of Pastor Lewis, I have questioned my motives more than once, but right now I need to keep my head in the game. Just when I think the game is over there is a sudden game change and I need to know what happened.

Forty-five minutes later we arrive at the church and I get out of Victory's car and hand her the keys.

"Do you want me to wait for you?" Victory says before she gets into the car.

"No, that's okay. I'll call you later." I turn around before Victory has a chance to reply. I need to get to this meeting right away.

I jog up the front steps and enter the church lobby. All of the lights are off except for the one by Pastor

Robinson's office. I walk over to Pastor Robinson's office and knock on the door.

"Minister Dungy?" I recognize Minister Blackwell's voice from the other side of the door.

"Yes, it's me."

Minister Blackwell opens the door and his face conveys that he is not happy to see me. I enter the office and notice that Pastor Robinson is in tears. This is not good.

"What did you do?" Minister Blackwell asks.

"My job," I reply.

"Your job. I can't believe this!" Minister Blackwell shakes his head.

"What happened?" I ask.

"You tell me, Mr. Clean. How did this happen?" Minister Blackwell fires back.

"Look, I don't have time for these guessing games. Either somebody tells me what's going on or I'll walk."

Pastor Robinson doesn't say anything; she just sits at her desk in front of her laptop with her hand over her mouth. Pastor Robinson's tears are still fresh when she turns her laptop toward me. I have seen a lot of disturbing things over the last few weeks, but these are images of a Web site that says Pulpit Sluts with a picture of Pastor Robinson holding a Bible on the left side, and on the right side is a video clip on rotation of Pastor Robinson from her days as a porn star.

"Who sent this?" I ask.

"You know who. He sent me an e-mail with this link. He says it goes out to the public tomorrow," Pastor Robinson says, not taking her eyes off the laptop even though the laptop is turned away from her.

"What did you do?" Minister Blackwell asks.

"I had a meeting with the CEO of Another Level Productions," I reply.

"That was not your job. Your job was to find First Gentleman Robinson and that was it. You brought this on her and for no reason."

"I needed to know if the money I was paid had any connections to First Gentleman Robinson's disappearance."

Minister Blackwell gives me a shove that catches me off guard. I fall back to the bookcase and knock down some unidentified objects. On a normal day Minister Blackwell wouldn't have tried me, but he is enraged. Even though I could take him in a fight, I am not about to test Minister Blackwell's resolve.

"You're going to make this right before it goes public or so help me God I will do a war dance on top of your head."

I have no doubts that Minister Blackwell would make good on his threats and there is one place I need to go in order to make this thing right.

Chapter Twenty-eight

"Reservation for Nicodemus Dungy." I hand my ID and printed reservation number to the same girl at the same rental car agency at the airport who handled my reservation when I first arrived. I'm certain that she doesn't recognized me, but I recognize the girl and the fact that she worked the night shift when I first arrived and now works an entirely different shift.

"Thank you very much. Your car is already waiting for you." The girl hands me my ID and the key information.

I head to the parking lot and find the Dodge Stratus. I get into the car and have no intention of forming a bond with the car. I just need to get to San Francisco and meet with Brian Perkins. The clock is ticking and we are behind on points. Perkins's move is a game changer. I was foolish not to see this play. I should've known that he would try to exact revenge but my judgment has been clouded by the first gentleman's disappearance and the serial killer who was at large. Now Perkins has the upper hand, but I have to steal it back.

I drive out of the parking lot and get onto the 80 freeway. Along the way I think about all of the possible things I can do to right the ship. I think about Pastor Robinson and her husband Tony Robinson. Their marriage hangs on by a thread and the last thing Tony needs is to be reminded why he left in the first place.

I also think about Victory and how I hope to see her again. When I was with Victory, I entertained another life. A life when I could trust a woman. My profession has left me skeptical, but this case caused me to believe that not everyone is looking to get over; some just want to be loved. I believe that Victory is such a person but I have a long way to go before I can be in that place where I can settle down. For now, I have to do the one thing that I am good at and that is fix things.

I arrive at Another Level Productions. This is the last place I want to be and I only have one play here to resolve this matter. The building looks closed for business, but there are a few lights on toward the top floor. I stand outside of my rental car and wonder whether Perkins is alone. If Perkins is alone then I might be able to sway him to drop this whole idea of exposing Pastor Robinson. If not then I have a whole other problem.

I walk to the front sliding doors and am not surprised when they do not open. I knock on the door and the security guard ignores me. I knock on the door again, and again the security guard does not respond. Perkins knows that I am on my way to see him so why didn't he alert the security guard? Moments later I see the security guard on the phone and when he hangs up the phone he finally acknowledges my existence and walks over to me and opens the door.

"Sorry about that," the security guard says.

I am sure he is not sorry, but right when I enter the hallway a large figure emerges. I am sure that before this guy accepted a position as one of Perkins's goons, he probably was a middle linebacker. I walk toward the individual with some trepidation.

"Right this way." The goon leads me into a lobby where we wait for the elevator to arrive.

When the elevator doors open I get onto the elevator and feel even smaller than before. While on the ride up, I think about the action movies I love to watch where the hero is in an elevator and then has this intense fight on the elevator. The hero overpowers the villains and then walks out of the elevator as calm as can be while the villains lie in the elevator, unconscious. But this is not an action movie and this guy can make me plummet to the ground.

We arrive at the floor where Brian Perkins's office is and this time I can hear loud music coming from the hallway. I head toward the office and the goon follows me and erases any notion of a retreat.

"It's open," the goon says.

I open the door and there is Brian Perkins in a two-piece suit with a cigar in his mouth. "Come on in, Preacher, and join the party."

I am reluctant, but then I enter the office and find that Perkins and two other goons equally as big as my goon escort were engaged in a film that starred Pastor Robinson. I shudder at the image and at the same time I am aroused by her sexual activity.

"Yeah, Preacher, I told you that she was one of the best, but you probably know that because when you're alone with her in her office, I bet she gives you your own private show."

"I'm here; now what do you want?"

"Well, isn't it obvious? I want the world to see what a hypocrite she is." Perkins points to the screen.

"Okay, turn that off." My words are drowned out by Pastor Robinson's moans. "Turn it off!"

Perkins pauses the movie, jumps up, and pivots around his desk. His goons follow him and my escort goon moves in behind me. The room gets a lot smaller.

"Don't be coming up in my office like you're John Gotti and ordering me what to do."

In a fair fight, I could take Perkins. But with his goons, the only thing I can do is take Perkins to dinner.

"Look, if you wanted to run with the Web site footage, then you would've by now. I think I know what you want and here it is." I go into my pocket and remove the envelope and extend it toward Perkins. "This is the $150,000 you gave Pastor Robinson. I'm giving it back to you in exchange for the footage you have on her."

After a moment, Brian Perkins starts to laugh hysterically. "Whoo wee, you must be used to dealing with amateurs. It's going to take a lot more than that to buy my silence."

"You said that this was the money that you owed her!" I say.

"And you believe that? I lost more money when she up and left."

"Look, take the money and let's put this behind us. She's changed her life and you obviously are doing better. Let it go and take the money."

Perkins takes a puff of his cigar and then he gives me a punch to the sternum. I fall to my knees and hear the sound of paper being torn. Then I can feel the heat of the cigar come close to my ear before a cloud of smoke is blown into my ear.

"I take no mess from a crooked preacher trying to be a gangster, and I'm not done with Li-Li until I see her whole sanctified world crumble. You heard me?"

That is the last thing I hear before I feel the sharp sting of wingtip shoes being kicked into my rib cage and my mouth. I try to cover up, but the blows get worse and the laughter gets louder. I then feel two strong arms pick me up and carry me out of the office. I am taken down the lobby to the elevator. I don't see the security guard and I assume that he is on break. While on the elevator I don't know if the goons plan to murder me or turn me loose. All I know is that I am glad that I don't have to worry about being kicked and punched.

Once off the elevator I am carried out of the lobby and through the parking lot to a car. I am leaned against the car and the final blow comes to my stomach and I fall back down on my knees.

"And that concludes tonight's Bible Study," one of the goons says.

It takes me awhile to get on my feet and I get in my car. I grimace as I reach to turn on the ignition. I struggle to get out of the parking lot and I struggle to drive on the highway. The pain from the blows is too much and I lose control of the car, and the car steers off the road before I lose consciousness.

Chapter Twenty-nine

Pain doesn't often get its just due. Pain often has a negative connotation to it. People try all kinds of ways to avoid pain, including death. For me, pain is an indicator that something is wrong and needs to be fixed. Pain also is an indicator that I am alive. I awake in the hospital full of pain. When I open my eyes Pastor Robinson and Minister Blackwell are there with their Bibles in hand.

"Never thought I would be happy to see you two," I say.

"Likewise. The last thing I need is for you to die," Pastor Robinson says.

I take a moment to assess my environment. I am hooked up to an IV and a machine that is monitoring my heart rate. My rib cage has been bandaged as well as my left arm. My face feels swollen and I can only imagine what damage was caused by Perkins and what other damage was caused by the car accident.

"You're lucky to be alive. The paramedics found the car on the side of the road, totaled," Minister Blackwell says.

"What happened?" Pastor Robinson asks.

"I went and saw Brian Perkins. I made him an offer and he refused."

Pastor Robinson shakes her head and walks over to the side of my bed where a container of water is positioned. She pours a cup of water and assists me in taking sips. "Did he crash your car?"

"No, I crashed it, but Perkins and his wonderful group of distinguished gentlemen did help."

"I'm so sorry," Pastor Robinson says. I can tell she is genuine and if nothing else this whole ordeal helps soften her shell.

"Listen, I'm not much for pity parties, especially when I'm the guest of honor. Has it gone online?"

Both Pastor Robinson and Minister Blackwell shake their heads in unison. I want to feel relief that the news about Pastor Robinson's other life has not been exposed, but something is up. Perkins wouldn't reveal his hand if he didn't expect to play it.

"He wants to meet with Pastor Robinson face to face."

"That's good isn't it? That means he wants to settle it." Pastor Robinson seems hopeful.

"Last night I offered him my complete fee. $150,000. If he rejected that, then I'm afraid his price is too steep."

I can see the concern on both Pastor Robinson's and Minister Blackwell's faces. I made a mistake in underestimating Perkins. If I am to resolve this issue, then I need to think a step ahead.

"Then again maybe not, but we don't have much choice in the matter. Set up a meeting and we'll go from there."

Pastor Robinson gives me a head nod and sets the cup of water down on the portable table next me. Pastor Robinson and Minister Blackwell pray for me and then they leave me alone to contemplate my position and how I can rise out of it.

I awake again in the hospital, still quite sore, but this time I see another familiar face.

"Before you say it, I did see the other guy and he got the better of you," Paul says with my Jell-O in his hands.

"Are you here for any other reason than to tell bad jokes and eat my Jell-O?"

"I told you I don't have many friends so when I get the word that my friend is in the hospital, well, that made me push my flight back."

I am glad to see Paul, especially for this next phase of my plan. The last few days in the hospital with heavy medication has forced me to sleep and as a result my mind is sharper than a samurai sword. I figure out a way to resolve this matter and Paul will play an intricate part in my success.

"So who did this to you?" Paul asks.

"Brian Perkins."

"Why is he not in handcuffs?"

"Because I have something much bigger in store for Mr. Perkins."

Paul grabs a seat and pulls it closer to me. I know I have his ear, which means that I have won half the battle of getting Paul to do exactly what I need him to do.

"I need you," I say.

"I figured that. What do you need?"

"I need to take down Perkins, and hard," I say.

"Why, because he's threatening to post some very interesting video footage of your pastor friend?" Paul sets the empty cup of Jell-O on the table next to me.

Paul is a great journalist, but his problem is that he doesn't know how to turn it off. Paul knows what happened to me, but he wants to first see the cards I am holding before he shows me his hand.

"She's a good woman. I've witnessed it first hand. She's an honorable woman and I need you to dig up whatever you can find on him."

"When I come across this information, should I bring it to you at the Bada Bing? Or maybe we could do like *Casino* and go out to the desert to talk. If you're going to be a gangster, then make sure you look the part."

"Don't start that." I wish I could walk away from Paul, but with limited mobility, all I can do is turn my head.

"Nic, you're in the hospital beat up. I've reported on a lot of things; from a woman who tried to stick her child in the oven because she said that God wanted a burnt offering, to a guy who drove drunk backward through downtown Los Angeles and didn't hit a single car. A preacher who gets beat up while supposedly preaching the Gospel ranks right up there."

"Look, Paul, we have plenty of time to discuss my life, but I need you to help me resolve this problem."

Paul heads toward the door and stops at the doorway. "I'll see what I can come up with. In the meantime you take care of yourself."

And like that Paul leaves and like that I drift back off to sleep.

Chapter Thirty

After two days of *Seinfeld* reruns, questionable hospital food, and a motley crew of nurses, I am discharged from the hospital. Nothing more major than a couple of bruises to my ribs, nose, arm, and most of all, pride. I call the one person I want to see the most, Victory. Victory shows up to take me back to the hotel. With the help of the nurse, Victory takes on the dubious honor of wheeling me out the hospital in a wheelchair. With my right arm in a sling, I can't do much but scratch my nose.

Victory wheels me out of the hospital into the open parking lot across the street from the hospital. I don't like to be vulnerable, but Victory is the one person who makes vulnerability tolerable.

"You're lucky to be alive," Victory says.

Victory helps me get into the passenger seat of the car. I grimace from the multiple bruises. I feel anything but lucky at the moment.

"It's by the grace of God that I'm alive," I say.

Victory closes the door and gets in on the driver's side. "Okay, we're going to stop at the store and pick up a few things and then go to your hotel to rest."

I have not told Victory where I stay. That is a firm rule that I am about to break, but do I have a choice?

"That's probably why you got into the car accident. You haven't had enough rest." Victory says.

That and a bunch of goons who decided to play soccer and use my body as the soccer ball.

"Where are you staying?" Victory asks.

"Executive Suites."

We drive along the highway and I watch the clouds swallow up the sun. For the first time I don't have a care in the world. I am not vexed by the Pastor Robinson situation or my injuries. I just watch the sun as my eyes close.

"Come on, sleepy, let's go inside."

Victory shakes me and I fully awaken in the parking lot of the Executive Suites hotel. I am still a little foggy from the medicine.

"Thank you," I say.

"Hold on. Let me come and get you." Victory gets out of the car.

"That's okay, I got it." I try to beat Victory by getting out of the car first and I almost fall down from being lightheaded.

"I told you; don't rush, I got you."

Victory takes my arm and throws it over her shoulder. Victory starts to assist me from the parking lot to the hotel. *My physical wounds will heal faster than my pride.* We head to the hotel entrance, but Victory does not stop there. She continues to assist me through the lobby and does not stop until we arrive at the elevators. Victory leans me against the wall to take a breath until the elevator arrives.

When the elevator doors open, I sneak into the elevator before Victory can help and I find a spot on the other side of the elevator.

"You think you're slick." Victory smiles. "What floor?"

I hold up the number three and Victory presses the button to my floor. Victory has a smile on her face. I wonder what makes her smile. We arrive at my floor and Victory resumes her responsibility of assisting me to my room. After a few fumbles I find my key and open the door. Victory lets go of me and I stumble to the bed and lie down.

"I'll be right back," Victory says as she takes the extra key off the table and heads out the door.

I lie on the bed with my eyes closed. I hear the door close and after a moment, I gather enough strength to get up and head to my briefcase. I take out a change of clothes and my toiletries. My left arm is being overworked, but I have to take a shower to wash off the hospital experience.

I go into the bathroom and set my things on the counter. I need to protect my bandaged arm from the water, so I grab the trash bag from the empty trashcan and I take my arm from my sling and wrap the plastic bag around my forearm.

It takes my body a minute to adjust to the warm water and I grimace from the pain and the exhaustion of having to do everything with my left hand. I hear the door open and close and realize that Victory has returned. I stay in the shower a few more minutes and I feel a lot better by the time I turn the water off. I want to avoid an awkward situation so I make sure that I get fully dress before I leave the bathroom. I have the most difficult challenge putting on my shirt with one arm.

I walk out of the bathroom and on the table is a nice spread of bread, vegetables, and meats. Victory is at work putting together a sandwich.

"How was your shower?" Victory asks with her back turned toward me.

"It'll suffice for now."

"Do you like mayonnaise?" Victory asks.

"Love it!" I sit down on the edge of the bed.

Victory finishes making the sandwich. She grabs a bag of barbeque chips from a grocery bag, opens it, and pours some chips onto the plate. Victory hands me the plate and I take it with my one good arm.

"Thank you," I say.

"No problem." Victory hands me a bottle of water. "It's not good to take pills on an empty stomach, so take a couple of bites and then take your medicine."

I follow the doctor's orders and eat half of my sandwich before I take my prescribed Vicodin. I sit on the bed and eat and Victory takes a seat in the chair next to the table and eats as well. I turn on the TV and we watch a rerun of *A Different World*.

"In high school my classmates use to tease me and call me Whitley."

"I wonder why?" I say in my most sarcastic tone.

My comment is rewarded with a balled-up paper thrown at my head. I finish my lunch and hand the trash to Victory. It doesn't take long for the Vicoden to kick in. I lie back in the bed and drift off to sleep.

A knock on the door wakes me and all that is left of Victory is her scent. That and a note on the table. While I am curious to know who is at my door knocking, I am even more curious to read Victory's note. I get up and walk over to the table. The knocking does not cease, which means that whoever is on the other side of the door knows I am home. I unfold Victory's note.

I enjoyed lunch and I figure I'd let you get some rest. Let me know if you need anything.

I smile, but another knock on the door reminds me that I have company. I pray that this is not one of Brian Perkins's goons coming to finish me off. I open the door from an awkward position with my left hand and there is Pastor Robinson on the other side.

"Minister Dungy, I'm sorry to bother you, but I really needed to talk with you."

How did you know where I stayed? I am off my game and that is not good. "Come on in." I open the door wide enough for Pastor Robinson to come in. Once she is in I close the door.

"How are you?" Pastor Robinson asks.

"About as well as can be expected. What happened?'

"Brian got in contact with me. He wants to meet on Friday." Pastor Robinson takes a seat in the chair that Victory sat in a few hours ago.

Time is relative when you've spent the last few days in the hospital. It takes me a moment to realize that today is Wednesday, which meant that we only have two days to prepare for this meeting. Lost in my thoughts I don't notice that Pastor Robinson has started to sulk.

"Pastor Robinson," I say to get her attention.

"I don't want to lose him! I love my husband and I don't want to lose him, but I don't have the strength to fight."

This whole experience has brought Pastor Robinson to her knees. I feel the same way and I think that it is only fitting that I help Pastor Robinson back to her feet.

I kneel down and face Pastor Robinson. "We may be pressed on every side, but we are not broken. We're going to get through this, but I need to get Tony on board."

Pastor Robinson looks at me skeptically, but little does she know that while I was in and out of consciousness I devised a plan that included the help of Tony Robinson.

Chapter Thirty-one

Pastor Robinson leaves shortly after our meeting. She left me alone to inhale Victory's scent and to contemplate a drink from the refrigerator. I experience mostly discomfort from my injuries but no real pain thanks to the medication. There is, however, a drawback to the medication. While the medication numbs the pain it also makes me less coherent and as a result not as sharp. I am still coherent and functional, but I am also out of it.

The meeting is set for Friday which doesn't give me a whole lot of time to recover. I could really use Jack Daniels. I open the refrigerator and I pulled out a little bottle of the infamous whiskey. I ponder how such a small thing carries so much power over me. I have been able to maintain my sobriety despite the crazy circumstances. I put the bottle back in the refrigerator and thus I regain some semblance of power and control.

While I wait for the Robinsons to show up, I turn on the TV and turn to CNN.

"The Husband Stalker. Two decades of terror," the narrator says.

Life is not without its coincidences. I just so happen to turn the TV on right when CNN is airing a documentary on the infamous serial killer. I know why CNN is doing this; because recently the Husband Stalker was apprehended by a bounty hunter and a preacher.

But the image of the psycho having his hands around my throat chills my blood, so I decide to turn the TV off and have a seat on my bed. The pain from my wounds and the image of the Husband Stalker ignite my desire to drink.

"Lord, I thank you for your grace and mercy, which strengthens me when I'm weak and empowers me not to give into temptation and drink." I conclude my prayer and feel a sense of relief.

A knock on the door signifies that the Robinsons have arrived. I get up off the bed and make my way to the door. When I open the door I find an eager Pastor Robinson and a reluctant Tony Robinson.

"Well, there's no time to waste, so why don't you come in and let's get started." I maneuver the door open to let both Robinsons in and close the door after Tony enters.

"No offense, but I was hoping not to see you again," Tony says.

"None taken," I say. I want to put my hands in my pockets, but my hands are still swollen.

"So what's up? Licia is being real secretive and I thought that we were past that," Tony says in reference to his wife.

"You guys will be, but there's one more thing we need to take care of. With God's help we can resolve this whole issue."

"So what do you need from me?' Tony asks.

"I'm going to get to you in a second, but right now I need to ask your wife something." I turn to Pastor Robinson. "Pastor, I need you to come clean about something."

"What?"

"I offered Brian Perkins $150,000 and he laughed in my face, but he didn't air the footage; why is that?"

The question may seem irrelevant to Tony, but it isn't to Pastor Robinson. Her face conveys that she knows exactly what I am asking her.

"When I was on camera I belonged to whatever man or woman they paired me with. When I was off camera, I belonged to Brian. When I left the industry, I also left him."

I thought I would feel relief from the revelation that Pastor Robinson did have a relationship with Perkins; instead I feel like the wind has been knocked out of me. Money problems are easier to solve than matters of the heart. With money it can be solved with money. All one has to do is agree on the dollar amount; that would rectify the situation. In matters of the heart one can be unreasonable and no amount of money could solve the problem. At this moment Brian Perkins could want anything from more money to Pastor Robinson leaving everything behind and coming back to him.

"Wow, your skeletons are really coming out now aren't they?" Tony asks.

"Don't start, Tony. This is hard enough."

Tony jumped up in a fit of rage. "No, forget that! It seems like every time I turn around, I am finding out something foul about you. I just want to know what you've done for these guys that you didn't do for me."

"You can't have it both ways, Tony. You can't have a lady in public and a freak in the bedroom," Pastor Robinson says.

"I'm not asking you to be a super freak, but I don't want you to be the iron maiden either. But I get it now. See I understand now that unless it's in front of the camera and I'm paying you boatloads of money then you don't know how to be intimate."

I expect a slap, but Pastor Robinson kicks Tony and then swings at his head. Tony shields himself from the heavy blows and I try to get in between but I end up stumbling over my own feet and I fall on the bed. A sharp pain rocks my whole body.

"Ministry Dungy, are you okay?" Pastor Robinson asks.

"I will be!" I pull myself up and go and have a seat in the chair next to the table. I take a moment to catch my breath. "Once you guys settle your differences."

"What do you want from me, Tony?"

"I want the respect I deserve. I've been a loyal, supportive husband to you. I've endured a lot of scorn and trash talking just so that you can be the next Juanita Bynum. All I ask is for you to show me the love and respect I deserve. Instead you continue to ask more from me and I'm not getting much in return. Now I got to forgive you for your past. Do you know how hard that is for me?"

"Yes, I do," Pastor Robinson says.

"You got your nerve. It's not like you were playing fast and loose in high school. You did porn. You slept with men for money and put it out there for the whole world to see."

"Yes, I did that! I did that because nobody was there to tell me different. I don't know the first thing about being in a relationship."

"So why marry me?" Tony asks.

"Because I love you and you were willing to love me."

I wrestle the pill bottle open to take a couple of pills to kill the pain. I see the sunken shoulders of Tony Robinson and I know that he has lost the stomach for further combat. I am sure Tony now wonders if the woman he fell in love with was based on false pretenses. He wouldn't have married Pastor Robinson if he had known her past, but there is nothing he can do about that now.

"Man, let's just hear the plan of how we're going to fix it," Tony says to me.

I stand up and I try to put my hands in my pockets. I at least get the Robinsons to talk about the tough road ahead. That is the easy part. The next part is to sell them on the plan that I have.

Chapter Thirty-two

The next day all I can think about is how my entire plan hinges on Paul being able to find something concrete. Paul has never come up short and I don't expect for him to now. At around noon I get a text message from Paul stating that he found something and that he is on his way. I reply to Paul's text with the directions to where I am staying.

The sling that once held my arm now causes more discomfort than comfort. I manage to get dressed with both arms and while I am still not fully recovered, I am at least past the eye of the storm. My face still looks like I have been in a bar fight, even though the swelling has gone down considerably. It takes me awhile, but I manage to put on my traditional gray suit with an open white collar shirt. I feel like a fraction of myself again and after Paul comes over with the information, I will need to get going with following up on a few leads.

Thirty minutes later I receive a knock on my door and it is Paul. He has a perturbed look on his face.

"When you get back to L.A. you're buying me dinner at Morton's steakhouse."

"I think I could manage that. Come on in." I open the door for Paul and close it as soon as he enters.

"I got him." Paul holds up the file and makes a beeline to the wet bar. He tosses the file on the table before he starts to fix himself a drink.

I walk over to the table and pick up the file. I rifle through a series of paternity suits, public fallouts with directors, and you name it. None of the information is reassuring me that Paul has gotten Brian Perkins right where I need him until I get to the end of the file and see a picture of a girl. The girl looks oddly familiar and it takes a moment, but I think I recognize the girl from when I first arrived and met with Pastor Robinson at the motel. This is the same girl who approached me as a potential client. It shows how small the world is.

I start to read the information attached and my heart aches with the gruesome details. "How accurate is this?" I ask Paul.

"Seriously?" Paul takes a sip of his drink.

I don't know why I bothered to ask. Paul's information is solid. He prides himself on journalistic integrity.

"If you need help I know a guy down at the precinct."

"Thank you," I say.

"Are you going to be okay with this?" Paul asks me.

"With the Lord on my side, there's nothing I can't handle."

Paul smiles despite having a mouthful of vodka. My plan starts to come together and there is one missing piece that will set the whole plan in motion.

The motel looks exactly the same as I remember it from two weeks ago. I thank God that my job allows me to change up the routine. As much as I bellyache about my job, at least the regimen of a different city and different problem to solve keeps me sharp and alert.

I go searching for the girl I met the last time I was here. Her face has been burned into my memory bank after reading her story and staring at her picture. It takes me a minute to spot her from all the other working girls who are leading their clients into the rooms. She wears a platinum blond wig, but her profile matches the profile of the girl, so I approach both her and her client.

"Sorry, boss, you're going to have to wait your turn," the client says before he looks at the girl. "Tell him, Roxy."

I reach into my pocket and pull out a knot of money. I peel off five one hundred dollar bills and extend them to the man.

"I'm not trying to cut; I just need ten minutes of the lady's time."

The man hesitates before he takes the money. I then set my sights on the girl. "And, Roxy, I'm willing to pay you a thousand dollars for ten minutes." I peel off ten bills and hand them to her.

"Ben, honey, let Roxy take care of this eager gentleman and then we'll party," Roxy says to her client before she puts the money in her bra. "Go wait in the car, daddy, until I go get you."

"Sure thing. Sweet thing!" Ben leaves and Roxy signals for me to follow her into the hotel room.

I follow orders and I close the door once we are both inside.

"You're not a cop, are you?" Roxy asks, to which I shake my head no. "Well, you paid for the time and you only got ten minutes. So let's get down to business."

Roxy starts to take her clothes off, and though she is tempting to look at, I have to resist. "That's okay. I don't want that, I just want to talk."

"Oh, you're one of those. Well, I don't know if I can give you a thousand dollars' worth of conversation."

"That's okay, because I want to talk about Regina Anderson."

If Roxy could turn white, she would. The name Regina Anderson stops her dead in her tracks.

"I don't know anyone by that name."

"Regina had dreams of being a movie star, so she moved to Hollywood to pursue her dreams of being an actress. But with the exception of a few parts as an extra, Regina got lost in the shuffle until she came across a director named Brian Perkins who wanted to make her a star."

"Why are you telling me this?" Roxy asks.

"Because I know what happened to Regina. I know and I want to help."

"You can't help me. No one can," Roxy replies.

"I don't believe that. I've seen a woman in the same situation as you rise above her situation and become an influential leader in her community. She became this woman because of Jesus and that same blood is able to cleanse."

Tears flood Roxy's face. I have broken the barrier and the worst thing I could do was talk her back into defensive mode. I let the silence sit in for a few minutes.

"Your time's up, mister."

"Now the same man who hurt you is trying to destroy this woman and I need your help."

There is a knock on the door. "Hey, time's up!"

It must be her client who is waiting outside. Roxy gets up and walks over to the door and opens it. "Look, honey, we're going to have to party later."

Roxy reaches into her bra and hands the money back to him. Roxy closes the door and takes off her platinum blond wig and tosses it onto the bed.

"I'm not the woman you think I am. I have made a lot of mistakes."

"Raven, (No inconsistency he was telling Roxy's story to try to get her to help him with Regina.) I read over your profile and story. Most of the things that happened to you are based on the poor perception that you have of yourself. You need to change your mind about yourself and see that you can do more."

"Why would God allow this to happen to me?"

"The Bible calls us to repent and that means to change your mind. To answer your question, God just needs you to have a mind change about yourself."

"What happens next?" Roxy asks.

"I'm going to get you into a program to help get you clean and when I need you I will call you." I head to the door.

"Wait."

I stop at the door and turn.

"You never told me your name."

"My name is Minister Dungy."

Roxy smiles at my statement. It feels good to be called Minister Dungy.

"Would you stay with me and talk to me about Jesus?" Roxy asks.

"I wouldn't be much of a minister if I didn't."

Chapter Thirty-three

I have two hours until the meeting and I need some insurance. I go over to Spider's place and I find him dressed in his bounty hunter uniform.

"Is this a bad time?"

"Not at all. I heard from your boy what happened. I would've been there, but I had this chance to track this person down and I was out of town."

"I need your help."

"I got you."

I am amazed at how Spider just came up on a big payday and he is still out there catching criminals. He hasn't skipped a beat with his job.

"Let me be specific. I need help from you and some of your friends."

"Are you sure?"

I'm not sure about anything, but I also know that things could go wrong in so many ways. To ensure a victorious outcome is to do something out the bone.

"Yeah, I'm sure," I say.

"Are you sure about this?" Pastor Robinson asks.

That seems to be the question of the day as I drive along the freeway with Pastor Robinson in the back seat and her husband in the passenger seat.

"I'm not sure about anything but we have to do something and this is my best play."

This is unfamiliar territory for me. I usually dictate the terms and dominate the conversation. I have to play my hand early.

Out of my peripheral vision I see Tony Robinson sitting there, quiet. "You all right, Tony?"

"Man, I'm just ready for this to be all over."

"I know and I just want you to keep in mind that this guy Brian Perkins is a scum bag and he will say anything to get you to react. Don't bite no matter what."

Tony does not respond and when I look back at Pastor Robinson she has her head down, engaged in a prayer. The life that Pastor Robinson tried to forget is staring her in the face and she needs to be ready to confront it.

I get off the freeway and work my way up the surface streets toward Brian Perkins's office. As we get closer, my stomach ties in knots. I am nervous and that is not a good sign.

When I pull into the parking lot of Brian's office, it takes me a moment to regain composure and turn off the ignition.

"Let's have a word of prayer," I say to the Robinsons. We pray and then exit the car. I start to walk toward the building and I think about how the last time I was here I was being dragged out, beat up. The fact that I'm returning to right a serious wrong gives me poise and makes me stand up tall.

I enter the building and the Robinsons follow me. I make no eye contact with the security guard because as far as I am concerned, the man is a coward. We get on the elevator and I vow that this will be the last time I ever get on this elevator again.

Just like last time, when I get off the elevator I can hear music from down the hall. I lead the Robinsons out of the elevator and to Brian Perkins's office, where a man opens the door and blows out a puff of smoke.

"We're here to see Brian."

"Let them in, fam," Brian says from behind his goon.

The goon steps aside and there is Brian sitting in his chair with his feet on his desk watching another movie starring Pastor Robinson.

"What up? Just watching my girl do her thing." Brian looks at Pastor Robinson, who is horrified. "Dang, ma, you done gotten chunky there. Still sexy though."

"I don't need your approval. I am beautiful and God has been good to me," Pastor Robinson says.

"Please; can't no God and no man treat you like I treat you." Brian takes a puff of his cigar.

I can feel the heat rise up on Tony. I put my hand on him to settle him down.

"I see you brought your man; yeah, I'm sure he ain't hitting that right."

"I ought to break your neck!" Tony says.

"Are preachers supposed to talk like that? Huh? What's a matter with you? You don't come up in a man's establishment and disrespect," Brian says.

"Be cool, Tony," I say.

"You better listen to your boy because he found out the hard way what happens when you disrespect me."

The anger inside me has reached a boiling point and I desperately need this plan to work.

"Stop it, okay, Brian? Just stop please!" Pastor Robinson fights back the tears. "I know I hurt you, but I had to get my life together. I could no longer destroy myself. Please forgive me."

Brian has a smirk on his face and I never wanted to smack a man so much in my life.

"Oh I forgive you, ma, but I won't forget. I won't forget all the money you cost me and how you played me. I gave you my heart and you walked away from it. But"—Brian pauses his movie—"we'll always have memories."

The men chuckle and I use that as a point to unplug the TV. The goons jump up and I don't back down. One of the goons steps up, but I don't back down and I feel Tony stand beside me, ready to fight. Hopefully it won't come to that because we are outnumbered, until I hear the sound of Harleys nearby.

"You don't learn do you, Preacher?'

"Apparently I do. You might want to check outside."

Brian gets up and looks outside and his whole demeanor changes. "Who are they?"

I walk over, and lined up in a row outside of Brian's office are bikers with Spider standing in the middle. I give Spider a head nod and he walks toward the entrance.

"They are your problem if we're not out of this building unharmed in ten minutes."

"Ten minutes?" Brian asks.

"Well, eight now that we are here, but I only need two minutes." I reach into my jacket and pull out an envelope and hand it to Brian.

"What's this?" Brian asks.

"This is the reason why you're going to hand over every piece of material you have of Pastor Robinson and shut down your Web site."

Brian reviews the material and tries to hand it back to me. "I don't know what you're talking about."

"Seriously, you've raped that many women that you can't recognize them? Regina has come forth and she plans to testify and I hope you like prison because that's where you're next movie is going to be filmed from, but I don't think you like your costars."

"Okay, so I drop the footage and this all goes away. Okay, I can do that." Brian's swagger has disappeared.

"You misunderstand me; you're going to drop the footage and then you're going to jail. I've already given this information to a detective who is on his way to arrest you for rape."

There is a knock on the door and Tony opens it. Spider enters the room in his bounty hunter suit complete with an array of weapons. He stands there imposing his will on the rest of the room. Brian crumples up the paper and tries to swing on me. I block his punch with my forearm and feel a sharp pain.

Tony Robinson leaps over the desk and punches Brian while Spider draws his weapon on the other goons. Brian is knocked out and I know that that feels good for Tony to knock Brian out.

"Dude, you're going to have to learn how to fight," Spider says.

"I guess you're right," I reply

I look at Pastor Robinson and she starts to laugh and then she starts to cry. It's an impressive display of emotions because the tears come from the pain of the past and the laughter of deliverance. "Thank you Jesus, thank you, you keep your promises!"

Chapter Thirty-four

I don't want to go back home. I am not sure if the apartment I have in Carson qualifies as a home. I feel more at peace and at home in Victory's Lexus than I feel anywhere besides church. Right now I wish that we could just keep on driving past the airport. Maybe we could go to Reno or maybe I could take her with me to Southern California. It is a fantasy and I know that, but every now and again I like to dream.

"You need a vacation." Victory adjusts the glasses on her head.

"When I was a kid, my father took me to Crooked Island Bahamas to meet my grandfather. I was only five and I vaguely remember the place, but I always wanted to go back there."

"So go. You need money for a plane ticket?"

I chuckle to myself because Victory has no idea that I am $150,000 richer. "No, I don't need any money, but I may need a companion."

"I may be able to swing that," Victory replies.

Being in the car with Victory reminds me that I can never have both a life and the job. The job requires me to be a different person and despite my best efforts, I can't turn my personality on and off like a switch. I can't help a pastor cover up an affair and then go home to sweet Victory and play happy home. I have to choose and at this point I have spent too much time in the muck to clean up for Victory.

"I'm thinking about heading down to Southern California. Maybe you could show me around. Take me to Hollywood, Disneyland, and Roscoe's Chicken and Waffles."

"Hollywood is overrated with a bunch of panhandlers. Disneyland is overpriced and only the Roscoe's off of Pico is good."

Victory laughs and I am somewhat irritated because even my best attempt to be a jerk comes off as charm with her. Victory pulls into departures and I do not want to get out of the car, but I have to go. I unbuckle my seat belt and get out the car. I open the door of the back seat and get out my computer bag and duffle bag. I'm sort of glad that my rental car was totaled, because I wouldn't have had a chance to ride with Victory.

"Thank you for everything," I say from outside of the car.

"See you soon," Victory says.

I don't know how to interpret Victory's statement, but the thought that this is not my last time seeing her makes me smile. I tap the car and head toward the door. I don't know if I will see Victory again, and maybe it's for the best. It's better to leave things perfect than to allow time and opportunity to reveal our flaws. I want to remember Victory as perfect even at the cost of not seeing her ever again.

I sit in my seat and I wait for the plane to depart. I am at a window seat and that's not like me. I am in the mood for some change and once I get home I plan to go on a vacation. I am officially out of the problem-solving business. I don't know what I am going to do with my life; all I know is that the problems of the church will have to be resolved by God. I plan to go somewhere and get back in touch with God.

"Excuse me, doc," a tall figure says.

I adjust my seat to make room for the passenger who will occupy the seat next to me.

"Thank you, bro. God bless!" I now get a good look at this individual and am surprised to see him on this flight.

"We might as well get acquainted since we're going to be on this plane together. My name is Titus Dawkins."

"I know who you are, Pastor Dawkins. You're the senior pastor of Greater Anointing."

"Have we met?" Pastor Dawkins asks.

No, we haven't, and you need to be thankful for that! Pastor Dawkins is an anointed minister, but there are rumblings that Pastor is a bit of a womanizer. Despite the fact that Pastor Dawkins fits the description of a womanizer with his good looks and thorough knowledge of the Word, the claims are baseless.

"My name is Nic Dungy and I'm a minister of the Gospel as well."

"So what church do you serve in?" Pastor Dawkins asks me.

"I go where I'm needed, Pastor. I don't serve in a particular church."

Pastor Dawkins lets out a groan and scratches his goatee. I know that Pastor disapproves of my answer, but I have no tolerance for being fake.

"So let me ask you this, Minister Dungy, who pours into you?"

"God pours into me," I say.

"I agree, but there should also be a fellow brother or sister in Christ who pours into you as well. Something tells me that you spend a lot of time traveling and helping other people and rarely do you consider yourself. A selfless man like you needs to have that love and devotion reciprocated."

I start to feel a little uncomfortable. Part of my success comes from no attachments. I am like De Niro in *Heat*. I don't allow any attachments that I can't walk away from at a moments' notice.

"Pastor, you and I are both in the recovery business. It takes a lot to help someone come out of darkness. It takes a lot to get people to see themselves the way that God sees them. I made a decision a long time ago that I was capable of reaching in and getting my hands dirty, but I was unwilling to burden someone with my filthiness in the process."

Pastor Dawkins does not respond to my question; instead he chuckles to himself. I am not known for my sense of humor.

"What?" I ask.

"Nothing, it's just that you are like me two years ago."

"Let me guess; you had a life-transforming experience."

"I did." Pastor Dawkins nods. "I found love and love always reminds you of your purpose and love always empowers you to continue you on that path."

Love: a word I often scoff at because it is a word said by too many selfish people. God is love and His work is selfless.

"If you're ever in the Long Beach area, you should come to Greater Anointing. We have a strong men ministry and every year we have an awesome men's retreat."

"We'll see," I say, but in truth I don't know if I would ever go to a men's retreat unless I had to.

Epilogue

Being from California, I'm used to the smell of sea water. Maybe it is a change of scenery or maybe it is the fact that for the first time in a long time I am not paying attention to the negative. I just allow the warm water to wash my feet and marvel at the fact that I can see my feet in the water. In front of me is open space. I find a secluded part of the island that is not tainted by Parasailors or jet skis. It is as peaceful as when God first created the island.

I have been in the Bahamas for a week now and I am not in a rush to get back to the States. Life is simpler out here and no one is in a rush. This is a perfect place for me to get back in touch with God. I need God to carry me through the transition. I haven't had a drink or a cigarette since Sacramento. I am in a good head space and I spend most of my days praising God with a clean heart.

I sent Victory an open plane ticket to come out. I don't know if she is going to come, but every day I watch the charter planes come in and drop off tourists and every day I feel a little disappointment that Victory has not shown up. I remind myself that it is better to remember her as a woman than anything else.

I take a sip of my drink and feel like a king. My drink is a mixture of passion fruit. And no alcohol. The sun rests easily on my shoulders, which is what one can expect during the first week of December.

I look off to my left and a short woman with a straw hat walks toward me. There is a bit of a wind so the woman has her hand over her head to keep her hat from flying off. As she gets closer I realize that it is Adele, the woman whose house I am renting while I stay out here on the island. I am not fooled by her miniature stature. Adele is one tough bird.

"You're going to stay out here all day?" Adele says with her thick island accent.

"Why not? I don't have days like this in L.A.," I say.

"I made lunch. Come get you something to eat."

I make it a point not to repeat myself and I also make sure that Adele does not have to repeat herself either. I start walking with her to the house, which is a beautiful beach house with a perfect deck.

"Oh, Lord," Adele says.

"What?" I ask.

Adele points to the road that snakes around the main hill. There is only one main road throughout this small island and there is a car travelling up the road.

"That's Prophet Chambers. He heads a church out here and he focuses on healing," Adele says.

"Okay, so what's wrong?"

"He's on his way to visit Mrs. Dixon, the wife of a prominent doctor out here."

I don't need any more clues to put together that Mr. Dixon is unaware that his wife will be visited by the prophet. Nor do I need to cut my vacation short and go back to work.

Readers' Questions

1. Do you think church problem solvers like Nicodemus Dungy exist?
2. Do you think Nicodemus Dungy is a minister or a cover-up artist?
3. Should someone who openly drinks and smokes cigarettes work in ministry?
4. Which scene was more powerful: Nicodemus praying for the entire church or him ministering to the prostitute?
5. Will Pastor Robinson and her husband Tony's marriage survive?
6. Does there exist a double-standard when it comes to women ministers?
7. What are your thoughts on the scene between Nicodemus and Pastor Dawkins?
8. Do you think Victory is going to meet Nicodemus on the island?
9. What potential clients could you see Nicodemus taking on in the future (fictional and/or real)?
10. Would you like to read another Nicodemus Dungy story?

UC HIS GLORY BOOK CLUB!

www.uchisglorybookclub.net

UC His Glory Book Club is the spirit-inspired brain-child of Joylynn Jossel, Author and Acquisitions Editor of Urban Christian, and Kendra Norman-Bellamy, Author for Urban Christian. This is an online book club that hosts authors of Urban Christian. We welcome as members all men and women who have a passion for reading Christian-based fiction.

UC His Glory Book Club pledges our commitment to provide support, positive feedback, encouragement, and a forum whereby members can openly discuss and review the literary works of Urban Christian authors.

There is no membership fee associated with UC His Glory Book Club; however, we do ask that you support the authors through purchasing, encouraging, providing book reviews, and of course, your prayers. We also ask that you respect our beliefs and follow the guidelines of the book club. We hope to receive your valuable input, opinions, and reviews that build up, rather than tear down our authors.

What We Believe:

—We believe that Jesus is the Christ, Son of the Living God.

—We believe the Bible is the true, living Word of God.

—We believe all Urban Christian authors should use their God-given writing abilities to honor God and share the message of the written word God has given to each of them uniquely.

—We believe in supporting Urban Christian authors in their literary endeavors by reading, purchasing and sharing their titles with our online community.

—We believe that everything we do in our literary arena should be done in a manner that will lead to God being glorified and honored.

We look forward to the online fellowship with you.

Please visit us often at *www.uchisglorybookclub.net*.

Many Blessing to You!

Shelia E. Lipsey,
President, UC His Glory Book Club

Notes

Notes